≈≈≈≈≈≈≈

"Scalpel. Scalpel. More scalpels. Wow. I didn't think I had this many..."

"Bone saw."

"Plaster saw."

"Splinter forceps."

"Rib shears, lobectomy scissors, and... Yeah, that's it." Still peering into the bag, I said, "I've got plenty salt for your wounds. I have these..." I held up a large mason jar. "I read some reports from that hospital you were in when you were a kid. Supposedly you're afraid of spiders. You still afraid of spiders?"

The tarantulas were huge but harmless. Totally domesticated, you could squeeze one half to death before it would bite, but Stabler didn't know that. He gasped and farted at the same time.

I returned the jar back to the bag, and he strained his neck trying to keep track of them.

I waved a hand in front of my face. "Goodness, man. If you're going to be farting, try to warn me next time. *Jeez.*" I rummaged through the bag a bit more.

"Well, that's pretty much it. I've got duct tape, vice-grips, a lead pipe, Vaseline... You know, the basics. Oh, and this." I lifted a brand new pair of pliers. "These are old-school, I know, but I like 'em." Finally, I removed a manila envelope from the bag and placed it on my lap. "You ready?"

"What do you want me to do?" he asked. He was scared and couldn't hide it anymore. I think it was the spiders that got him.

I removed a photo from the envelope. It was large, 8 by 11 inches, so I didn't have to hold it too close. I showed him the picture. "This is Lacy Rivers, your first victim."

He barely glanced at the black and white photo.

"Did you kill her?" I asked.

≈≈≈≈≈≈≈

PLAN C (AND MORE KWB SHORTS)

PLAN C
(AND MORE KWB SHORTS)

KEITH THOMAS WALKER

KEITHWALKERBOOKS, INC
This is a UMS production

KEITHWALKERBOOKS

Publishing Company
KeithWalkerBooks, Inc.
P.O. Box 331585
Fort Worth, TX 76163

For information write
KeithWalkerBooks, Inc.
P.O. Box 331585
Fort Worth, TX 76163

ISBN-13 DIGIT: 978-0-9850500-8-5
ISBN-10 DIGIT: 098505008X
Manufactured in the United States of America

First Edition

Visit us at www.keithwalkerbooks.com

*This book is for Anthony Douglas
Thanks for reading these stories
and giving me a great idea.*

*Congratulations to Phyllis Allen,
winner of the KeithWalkerBooks
short story contest! Read Phyllis' winning
entry, "Scenes From a Marriage,"
on page 136 of this novel.*

MORE BOOKS BY
KEITH THOMAS WALKER

Fixin' Tyrone
How to Kill Your Husband
A Good Dude
Riding the Corporate Ladder
The Finley Sisters' Oath of Romance
Blow by Blow
Jewell and the Dapper Dan
Harlot
Dripping Chocolate
The Realest Ever
Jackson Memorial

Visit keithwalkerbooks.com for information
about these and upcoming titles from
KeithWalkerBooks

ACKNOWLEDGMENTS

Of course I would like to thank God, first and foremost, for giving me the creativity and drive to pursue my dreams and the understanding that I am nothing without Him. I would like to thank my wife for being my first and most important critic, and I would like to thank my mother for always pushing me to be the best I can be. I would like to thank Janae Hafford Hampton for being the best advisor, supporter and little sister a brother could ever have. I would also like to thank (in no particular order) Jody Thomas, Brandy Rees, Denise Bolds, Sabrina Scott, Dianne Guinn, Kierra Pease, Jason Owens, Trey Williams, Keisha Mennefee and Uncle Steven Thomas, one love. I'd like to thank everyone who purchased and enjoyed one of my books. Everything I do has always been to please you. I know there are folks who mean the world to me that I'm failing to mention. I apologize ahead of time. Rest assured I'm grateful for everything you've done for me!

PLAN C (AND MORE KWB SHORTS)

CONTENTS

PLAN C (AND MORE KWB SHORTS)

GOING CRAZY

Marcus Ware hopped off the last step, and (much to the chagrin of the bus driver) leapt into an impromptu commando dive. With his backpack slapping his back and his arms extended, he rolled into a somewhat legitimate somersault. Next to art, gymnastics was Marcus' favorite hobby. From books he checked out from the library, he taught himself how to throw his body into the air with uncanny agility. Even better, he managed to land on his feet a great deal of the time.

If he lived on the *other* side of town, where they had big houses with manicured lawns and pretty street names, he might have asked his mother to enroll him in a gymnastics class that would nurture his God-given talents. But Marcus understood that his two member family was considered *upper lower class*.

Marcus lived in Overbrook Meadows' worst ghetto. There were more potholes in his neighborhood than promise. He would no more expect enrollment in a gymnastics class than he would expect a new pair of jeans in the middle of the school year. Certain things were simply too ridiculous to even ask for.

The airbrakes disengaged noisily, and the school bus drove away without any reprimands from the driver. What was she going to say anyway? Today was the last day of school. In a couple of months, when the blistering heat waves of summer began to ebb and the leaves finally began to show the effects of their daily baking, Marcus would start school again as a man. No longer a measly maggot with more boogers than good sense, he would be a sixth-grader. The time for fun and games had come to an end. He reminded himself of this as he righted himself and brushed the dead grass from his clothing.

PLAN C (AND MORE KWB SHORTS)

The Turners had a nice, soft lawn. It was great for tumbling, but they rarely raked after mowing. Marcus would have to take off his shirt and shake it out when he got home. His mother was a loving, patient woman, but she could be really anal about unnecessary messes like blades of grass on the couch.

Marcus walked two blocks with his heart light in his chest, and he turned left onto Forbes Avenue. From that intersection, there was only a six block trek to his home. Those six blocks were quiet, especially during the afternoon hours, but his mother worried about this part of his day more than any other. This was the only time Marcus was in the wide-open world with no supervision.

Marcus didn't see how anything could happen to him in the few minutes it took to get from the school bus to his front door, but the city's homicide rate was getting out of hand. Last year, there were over three-hundred bodies bloodied in the fair city of Overbrook Meadows. According to Marcus' mother, that meant one person got killed almost every day. There were a lot of gangs in the city, and they were clearly the biggest contributor to the violence. But Marcus didn't hate them like his mother did. In fact, he felt more fascination for the vermin than angst.

You keep thinking they cool, 'til you come home one day and they done broke in our house.

That was his mother talking. Even halfway across the city, Marcus' mom could chastise him. She wasn't a genius when it came to books, but Sonya Ware had more common sense than a class full of grad students. There were few circumstances she hadn't experienced and virtually no subject she didn't have an opinion on. Her opinion as of late was that black people needed to get their shit together.

Even though she was of African descent herself, Marcus' mom did not agree with a lot of things black people did. She had a view of her race, and she shared it with her son often: According to Sonya, there were black people, there were *niggers* and then there were *niggas*. Black people did well in school, got good jobs and took care of their kids. Black people were high in numbers, but their good deeds were often overshadowed by their counterparts. The *niggers* were the ones who would rather cash welfare checks than work for themselves. *Niggers* were too lazy to be much of a threat to the system politically, and they made black people look bad on a daily basis.

Niggers were bad, but *niggas* were the ones Marcus was supposed to watch out for. *Niggas* were the rapper, drug dealer types. The media had taken a liking to *niggas* for the past decade. They glamorized them, even though *niggas* were the thugs who were responsible for most of the things white people hated about blacks.

Niggas were the ones getting high, having sex without protection and providing drugs and alcohol to their toddler nephews. *Niggas* went to high school football games with their guns and would shoot into a crowd if they saw one person they considered an enemy. *Niggas* liked to deal drugs. They liked to get rich quick, get locked up and try to get rich quick again when they got out.

Sonya's number one beef with niggas was their cockroach mentality. They hung out in large groups. They preferred the dark, and they scattered when the police lights came on. Niggas liked to join gangs, and (like roaches) gangbangers don't die. They multiply.

Gang life sent two of Sonya's brothers to the penitentiary. A few of Sonya's girlfriends became single parents due to gang violence. Sonya would do anything to keep her only child away from gangs, but the best job her G.E.D. could offer didn't pay enough to put her on Alta Mesa Boulevard or Fossil Ridge Circle.

Not only was Sonya stuck in the ghetto, but a fresh crop of undesirables had moved in right across the street from her. They hung out and smoked marijuana all day. They sold dope and had no productive goings-on that Sonya had ever seen. Over the past four months, she called the police on them multiple times, but they were still there. Marcus saw them when he reached his block.

J.T. Elder Elementary was forced to initiate a dress code a couple of years ago. This was largely due to a sudden increase in fights at lunch and after school on almost a daily basis. Back before the dress code, a lot of kids came to school in solid red or green tee-shirts. Some of them even sported red or blue shoestrings with colored handkerchiefs dangling from their back pocket. Now the grade-schoolers could wear white, blue and khaki colors only. Marcus tried to wear a blue top and blue bottom as much as possible. He was glad he had done so on this particular day, because the gangsters on Forbes Street were Crips, and Marcus knew that Crips like blue.

There were three ruffians posted on or around the porch of the brown and tan house across the street from Marcus'. They never harassed or accosted their prepubescent neighbor, but Marcus thought it would be rewarding if he could get them to at least acknowledge him. He didn't necessarily want to be in their gang, but he did want a little recognition.

From what he'd heard, gangs were supposed to start recruiting youngsters around his age. He wouldn't join if asked, but Marcus took their disregard as a type of rejection. They lived directly across from him for the past four months. They watched him come and go to school five times a week – not to mention the many times he found some excuse to be in the front yard – but they never so much as nodded in his direction. Marcus hoped for more today as he stepped a little slower now, wearing all blue.

Marcus' interest in his neighborhood gang was a mystery, even to himself. He knew it had a lot to do with his mother's protective nature. But it had a lot to do with his dad, too. Having never met his father or grown up with any facsimile thereof, Marcus had a certain void growing within him. It was an elusive void. He couldn't touch it or pinpoint exactly what was lacking.

At the tender age of ten, it never occurred to Marcus that a teacher, a coach or even a scruffy dog could help fill his void, nor was he aware that juvenile detention centers were packed with little boys just like him who had similar voids. In fact, Marcus didn't even know he had a void. He only knew that the black males across the street had something that he had never seen outside of television: They had power. They were respected, feared and dangerous. They were the neighborhood superstars. The one with the big afro was like Snoop Dogg.

Marcus liked the one with the afro the most. He didn't know any of their names, but that guy would have a cool name like *Loc T* or *G Roc*. He would be the leader of the gang. He would be the one who got everyone excited about their crimes, and he would be the one who supplied everyone with weed. Marcus didn't know much about marijuana, but he had seen the guys across the street smoking it. Marcus thought the Crip with the afro was one of the coolest people he had ever seen. Loc T (or G Roc) wasn't the biggest, but he was the tallest. He kept a blue comb sticking out of his hair. Marcus had seen Loc T (or G Roc) get into an argument once, and the other guy backed down pretty quickly.

He wondered what would happen if he spoke to the gang across the street. They were a lot older than him, but he saw some younger boys over there from time to time. He knew that what he was thinking was absurd. His mother would skin his hide if she knew. But getting the Crips to notice him was getting to be a nagging desire. It was a pesky, four month obsession that would come to a head today. By the time Marcus reached his home, he had built up enough courage to initiate the encounter. He wouldn't go to their yard. He wouldn't ask them a bunch of stupid questions. He would merely say hello.

What up, cuz? Marcus knew that was how Crips acknowledged each other. They called each other "*cuz*," and they said things like, *What up, cuz*, or *What it was, cuz*, as a greeting.

"*What up, cuz?*" Marcus practiced under his breath. It sounded good. They would have to respond to that. They would say, "What's up," back to him. Maybe they would ask him something about school. He was good at math. Maybe they could talk about that.

Suddenly very giddy, Marcus stepped onto his porch and fumbled for the key looped around his neck. He kept his back to the Crips because he knew they were watching him, and keeping a key around your neck was something babies did.

Once inside, the first thing Marcus did was turn the air conditioner on. The house always felt like an oven when he got home from school. His mother wouldn't be home for three hours, but if Sonya did show up early and catch him in the front yard, he could just tell her that he was getting some fresh air. What mother wouldn't want her child to get fresh air?

Marcus squirmed out of his backpack and dropped it in the hallway on his way back to the front door.

≈ ≈ ≈ ≈ ≈ ≈ ≈

Bernard Sanders returned the lighter to Cory and watched him closely to see what kind of magic might be involved. Cory simply put the lighter in his front pocket. That was it. That was the big deal. Bernard had been wondering how Cory kept the same Zippo lighter for nearly six months. The average lifespan of a lighter in the hood was about one day. Bernard thought Cory had some special secret for keeping up with his, but it was merely responsibility this whole time. Responsibility was boring.

Bernard sucked hard on the Swisher Sweet cigar. It was stuffed with marijuana but poorly done. It was packed too tightly in some places and too loosely in others. It had at least three air leaks. It was obvious that Jamal had rolled the blunt. Jamal was only fourteen, and if it was up to Bernard his little ass would be in school, but he was Monty's brother, so he was cool.

Their set was small, but Monty maintained complete control over the members, and everyone was loyal. If Monty wanted his little brother to skip class and hang with the homies, then that's what happened. Bernard would be damned if his little brother would be hanging at a dope house, though.

Actually, the brown and tan house on Forbes Street wasn't a true dope house *per se*. They did manufacture crack at the location, but it wasn't an all night spot that would attract a lot of junkies. The cookies they baked were sold by the ounce, so their customers were dealers rather than users. Their customers were discreet and didn't come by without calling first. Monty's gang didn't make the best dope in the city, but it was better than average. They had buyers who would only score from them.

It only takes one person to cook crack, but there were always at least five people at Monty's crack house. This was mainly a security issue, but it was also good for camaraderie. The delinquents in this house all wore blue, and they all hated and loved the same people.

Bernard liked to be at the crack house because that's where the money was. And if you hang around the money, you're bound to have a good day. Whatever recreational drug you're into was always plentiful, and when unexpected windfalls came about, you'd be right in the midst of it. A dope fiend brought a hot Lexus to Monty's spot two weeks ago, for example, and he left it for only two hundred dollars worth of crack. And they currently had a female in the back room who'd been sucking and fucking for three days straight with hardly any food or sleep.

Monty had soldiers scattered throughout the city, but everyone knew that his Forbes Street spot was the place to be. Everyone there was like a blood brother. If someone came starting shit, they would get dealt with promptly and unanimously.

There were three members of the Sicc Crips on the front porch that day. Cory reclined in a metal folding chair with his back against the window sill and his feet barely touching the pavement. Cory was only 5'3", but he was as stout as a polar bear. He was dark skinned, 21 years old, with massive arms that could choke the life out of an anaconda. Cory had a large gap between his front teeth, like Mike Tyson, and he was rarely tested on the streets. Looking at him, most people would rather slap their mother than go one on one with the slugger.

Quincy loitered in the front yard dressed in blue and black. Quincy was a good guy, but he was the only member of their gang whom Bernard wouldn't trust with his life. Quincy was 38, almost a dinosaur in gangbanger years, but he didn't have the heart of a warrior.

Bernard had sat next to him during a driveby two months ago, and he watched Quincy's eyes grow wide with terror when the enemy shot back at them. Quincy dropped his gun on the floorboard, picking it up afterwards as they sped away from the scene. Bernard didn't report this, but he and Quincy locked eyes in the car. Bernard labeled him a coward, but he kept his mouth closed. Cowards are always found out in the end, and Bernard wasn't the snitchy type.

Bernard was the third person in the front of the house. He took the pick from his hair, fluffed out his afro, and watched the street as he tried to make sense of the blunt he was passed. Normally you could apply saliva to the problem area of a badly rolled cigar, but this one was ruined beyond repair.

There was a kid across the street wearing all blue. He used a key around his neck to gain entry into his home, which he shared with his rather attractive mom. Bernard had been watching the house for a couple of months, and he had the kid and his mom's schedules memorized. He wanted to break in one day, but Bernard didn't think he would find anything valuable. The mother drove a beat-up Chrysler to work, and the boy's shoes were all from Wayless.

It wasn't like the break-in would generate a cornucopia of suspects, either. The kid's mom had obvious disgust for the people in the house across the street, and if anything ever happened to her piece of shit shack, she would surely send the police straight to the Sicc Crips. That might fuck up their business for the day or the week, so Bernard procrastinated on the B & E.

The boy disappeared inside the house. Bernard watched for a few moments more, almost in a daze. He was thinking about the boy's mother. She was a light-skinned chick with nice, thick legs. Bernard liked big hips and thighs. Some of the homies thought she was a little chubby, but there was absolutely nothing wrong with Sonya in Bernard's opinion.

When they first moved in across from her, he used to have dirty daydreams on a regular basis. He would post up on the porch at six o'clock and wait for her to get home from work. On days she wore pants, his face would register disappointment. But his neighbor wore skirts more times than not. Bernard would stare at her calves, thighs and booty as she stepped the few paces from her car to the front door.

She caught him looking at her at least once, and she didn't register disgust with his voyeurism. Bernard thought she liked him, too, and if he could summon the courage to talk to her, she might be receptive to his charms. If she needed money, which she clearly did, he could help her out. He didn't like her runt very much, but he could get the kid some new shoes every now and then. Hell, if she let him tap that ass a few times, he would get the little motherfucker a new pair of Jordan's – every month.

Caught up in yet another fantasy about the big-booty sister across the street, Bernard neglected the one task – the *only* important task he had that day. This was a house used for manufacturing drugs. If someone robbed them, they would come into a financial windfall of epic proportions. Security was a necessity, not a luxury.

By the time Bernard looked up towards the sound of screeching tires, the two-toned Caprice's windows were down, and a gunman was propped out of the back seat holding a dark-colored pistol in each paw. Another shooter leveled what appeared to be a Mossberg pump from the front passenger window. Both shooters had black bandanas tied over the bottom of their faces. Both shooters had their eyes set on murder.

Bloody, bloody murder.

The barrage was immediate and deliberate. Bernard barely had time to tell his homies that, *"IT'S A HIT!"* and they needed to *"GET DOWN!"* before the block exploded with the sounds of war.

Intermingled with the ***POP! POP! POP!*** of the small caliber handguns was the deafening ***BOOM!*** from the shotty.

BOOM!

BOOM! BOOM!

Bernard reached instinctively to his waistband where he kept a weapon of his own. The .380 automatic was chrome with a black pattern on the handle. It glistened in the sunlight as it escaped the oppressiveness of his clothing and the muzzle got a taste of fresh air. The gun felt good in Bernard's hand, as if this is what it wanted.

This is what it always wanted.

The Caprice was moving slowly. Whoever the driver was, he was a good one. Most wannabe wheel-men get spooked by the sound of the first gunshot and slam their foot on the gas pedal. But this guy was cool. The Caprice crept like a leopard stalking. No scare tactic here. They wanted to make sure they bodied someone.

With gun in hand, Bernard felt a little better about his chances. But his outlook was still grim. The saliva dried up in his mouth, and his voice box clicked in his throat. So many heartbeats. So many bullets coming in his direction. The hair on the back of his neck was frigid. Every muscle was tense. Rising to his feet, Bernard cocked the chrome piece as something like a bee stung his cheek. The bite was quickly followed by the sound of a tiny, fiery missile bolting past his ear.

Backing towards the front door, Bernard leveled his pistol at the two-toned Caprice and began to let his own hot rocks fly. This was a moment that would forever live in gang folklore. It would be Sicc Crip history. The majority of people, even hardened criminals, will choose to duck when fired upon. It takes a *real nigga* to shoot back. This action would surely skyrocket Bernard's status among his peers. This was the shit legends were made of. This is how ghetto stars were born.

Bernard would blame Quincy for what happened next. He would regret remaining silent when Quincy failed them during a driveby two months ago. Bernard squeezed off shots as fast as his trigger finger could pull. He was only halfway through his clip when a hard body rolled into his legs. So eager to save himself, Quincy dove towards the porch, unwittingly bowling over their only defender. As he and Bernard fell into a crumpled heap of long arms and legs, Bernard let off two more shots. One of those bullets was Chuck.

Chuck was mad as hell.

And he wasn't bullshitting.

≈≈≈≈≈≈≈

Chuck was born two years ago in Raleigh, North Carolina. He wouldn't say that he was *born* hating people, but he would be the first to admit that his birth was saturated with destructive tendencies. Just days old, he had a good deal of cordite stuffed right under his butt. Beneath the cordite was a primer. His innards were held together with something his manufacturers called a *casing*.

Chuck didn't like his casing. Casings are the bitches of the bullet world. Casings were the snitches, the detective's dreams. They were the weakest link, and from the moment the casing was squeezed around him, Chuck wanted nothing more than to be free of it.

His full name was Semi-Jacket Hollow Point, but who wants to go by all of that? Even the shortened version, SJHP was a bit much for his tastes. *Chuck* suited him just fine, so he took that name for himself. When you're a bullet, you can pretty much take whatever you want for yourself. Chuck was actually the name of the first inspector to caress him, hold him, and verify him a success.

Chuck was placed in a box with twenty of his brothers, and this box was placed inside a larger box that contained fifty more boxes of twenty. The time spent in that box measured only months, but it felt like an eternity to Chuck. Some of his companions warned him to embrace the peacefulness and the tranquility of the box, to hope that he *never* got out of the box in fact, because when the box opened, he would die.

But what was that shit about? Chuck, as well as every other bullet in his box, was born to die. The projectiles were starting to sound like casings in that box, so Chuck was elated when it was finally opened.

Unfortunately, Chuck found that he was not in Iraq, but in something called a *sporting goods store*. He got this news from WSSM, a Winchester Super Short Magnum who said he had been there for at least six months. Six months was another eternity, but Chuck bid his time. While waiting, he got next to a Walther P99 pistol who claimed to have bodied at least seven people. Chuck also met a Colt python who had never been fired.

When his time to shine finally came, Chuck was ready. A young socialite bought the box he was in one broody winter morning and promptly stuffed him into the clip of her brand new handgun. Chuck was six of eight and feeling great. The socialite's purse was stolen three months later, and Chuck found himself the property of a dopefiend named Marty.

Marty was a fool. He never considered using Chuck to get all the drugs he wanted. Instead, Marty immediately traded the whole .380, Chuck included, to a lanky dealer named Lennox for a $30 piece of crack.

Lennox was small time. He bought his working dope from a house on Forbes Street. One month after landing the piece, Lennox sold the .380 to Bernard for seventy dollars. Chuck had to wait only six days before Bernard had use for him.

As Chuck zipped through the air – his ride lasting only a fraction of a second – his heart filled with an elation only lottery winners could understand, he allowed himself a moment to contemplate life, loss and the meaning of it all. He decided he didn't give a flying shit about any of that as long as he hit flesh.

He hit bone instead.

Chuck slammed into Marcus' head just above the right eye and skated through his brain like a mini rocket, taking a good deal of whatever he touched through a ping pong ball-size hole he created on the way out. With momentum ebbing, Chuck continued his route out of the back of the boy's skull, through Sonya's front door, and he came to a splintery stop in a kitchen cabinet.

Beat, battered, and horribly misshapen, Chuck was forced to consider the brevity of his task compared to the painstakingly dull wait he endured. As he cooled, he decided it had all been worth it.

Oh yeah, totally fucking worth it.

≈ ≈ ≈ ≈ ≈ ≈ ≈

Bernard rubbed the bruise on his cheek tenderly. There was a lot of blood. It snaked down the side of his neck and under his shirt collar. The whole side of his face was on fire.

"Get off me!" he barked at Quincy who was still cowering on top of him. Quincy lifted his head from Bernard's crotch and looked around anxiously.

"What?"

"I said get off me, *fool*! They gone." Bernard tried to stand, but he couldn't get the leverage with Quincy's body draped over his legs. He pushed with his free hand and delivered a rough knee to his friend's midsection.

"Get up, man! Monty!" Bernard called into the house. "*Monty!*"

"What's happening?" a voice from inside shouted.

"We got hit!" Bernard yelled.

Monty appeared in the doorway and looked around cautiously, taking in the scene. He had an SKS in his hands.

Quincy finally sat up and allowed Bernard to get to his feet.

"Who was it?" Monty asked. His grip on the weapon was super-tight, and he had not yet stepped outside. Bernard took note of all of this just as a young lion studies the dominant male.

Monty was tall and muscular. He had the body of a basketball player but never spent enough time in school to make a team. He was fair-skinned and handsome with a thick moustache he'd been sporting since puberty. At 23, Monty held the Sicc Crips together with the power of the almighty dollar. Money had always been the basis of his and Bernard's relationship. Money over bitches and money over beefs.

"I don't know," Bernard said. "I shot back, though." It was important to establish these things early on.

"Yeah, he did," Quincy piped in. Hoes always want to stay on your good side.

Monty stepped out onto the porch with his little brother Jamal trailing close behind.

"Damn, you got shot?" Jamal asked Bernard.

"Your shit's fucked up," Monty agreed, studying Bernard's cheek wound. "Where they go?"

Bernard ran his fingers across his bruise and flinched. "I don't know," he breathed. "They went around the corner. I think they went right. *This* nigga fell all on me!" He gestured angrily in Quincy's direction. "Where Tay?"

"He in there, getting the shit together," Monty said. "We gotta get outta here. You know them laws coming." He looked around the porch. "Cory dead?"

Bernard hadn't noticed before, but Cory was lying on the porch face down. A large puddle of blood was beginning to pool around his abdomen. His lips were almost flat on the concrete, but they blew no dust. No rise and fall of the shoulders, either.

"Damn," Bernard said and crouched next to the body. "Cory." He spoke softly, as if this was simply a mid-afternoon nap his friend was taking. "Cory," he said a little louder, nudging the man's shoulder this time.

"Tay!" Monty called into the house. "Hurry up! Get that shit together! We gotta go! Cory hit, cuz! Flush that shit if you have to!"

"Cory dead?" Tay called from within.

"*Cory!*" Bernard shouted close to the dead man's ear.

"You alright, Bernard?" Jamal wanted to know.

"This is fucked up. This shit's fucked up." Monty paced the porch, breathing quickly. "You don't know who it was?"

Quincy shook his head.

"Naw," Bernard said rising to his feet. He looked down at the 21 year old crumpled on the porch. He nudged Cory's leg with his sneaker. This *was* fucked up.

"Come on, man! We gotta go!" Monty shouted again. He was almost frantic. He grabbed Bernard by the shoulder. "Come on, cuz. You gotta go, too. You shot back?"

"Yeah," Bernard said, looking down the street from whence the shooters had come. There were a few neighbors outside now. They stood on their porches, eager to see what kind of trouble the Crips got themselves into now.

An elderly woman across the street and two houses down stood on the porch with her husband. She wore an old, blue robe. Bernard noticed that one of the robe's major buttons was missing. The fabric was pulled taut around her chest, and Bernard thought he could make out the nipple on one of her sagging breasts. Most of the neighbors were looking towards the dope house, but this lady wasn't. She was looking *and pointing* to a house on the same side of the street as hers. Bernard followed her gaze, and that's when he saw the boy.

Quincy must have been watching her, too, because he said, "*Daaamn*," just as Bernard was thinking the same thing.

Seeing the Caprice with shooters hanging out of the windows was a ghastly sight, but that was nothing compared to what Bernard felt when he saw the grade-schooler splayed out in his front yard. Bernard felt something sick and horrid pump from his chest and into his veins. His jaw muscles went slack, and he put his gun away.

"What happened?" Monty asked following their gaze.

Jamal took a few paces into the front yard, and he spied the body across the street, too. He looked back at his brother. "He dead?"

"What happened?" Monty asked again. He was looking at Bernard this time. His mouth was asking *What happened?*, but his eyes were asking *What did you do?*

"They shot him?" Jamal asked. His eyes were wide. He didn't look like a soldier who posted up in the dope house with a 9mm in his lap. He looked like a fourteen year old boy now. A scared little baby.

Yeah, Bernard thought. *They shot that kid. You see that? You see how fucked up people is today? They didn't have no reason to kill that nigga, except he did have on all that blue. Yep, they musta thought he was wit us. That's fuuucked up...*

"Bernard shot him," Quincy said timidly.

Bernard swung because he knew it was true. There was no way anyone but Bernard shot that little kid. No one in the Caprice was shooting in that direction. Bernard's left hook caught Quincy off guard and sent him sprawling in the grass. No one immediately did anything, so Bernard mounted the coward and unleashed a good, old-fashioned ass-whooping.

"*Fuck you!*" Bernard screamed as he pummeled his comrade. "It's your fault! *You* made me do it! You a bitch ass nigga! We never shoulda kept your ass around!"

Quincy cowered almost in a fetal position and tried to protect his face.

"Bernard!"

"He made me do it! He ran in–"

"*Bernard!*" Monty punctuated his shout with a shove.

Falling sideways, Bernard caught his balance and avoided rolling in the grass. He stood with fist balled, breaths heavy and blood leaking from his face and knuckles.

"He made me do it!" Bernard cried. He rushed in for one last kick, but Monty stepped between him and Quincy and pushed Bernard away.

"Get outta here!" Monty ordered. His eyes were stern, but they softened when he spoke again. "Cuz, you gotta get outta here. You gotta go, man."

And Bernard knew that was true. There was a dead kid across the street and plenty witnesses. He gave Quincy one more glare, the hardest look he could muster, and he resisted the urge to kick him in the head as he ran by.

Bernard heard the first siren as he rounded the corner onto Bright Avenue. Six blocks down the road, Bernard realized he lost his gun somewhere. The tobacco and marijuana damage in his lungs would catch up to him soon, so for now he gave it all he had.

Bernard ran like the devil himself was in pursuit. His feet clapped the pavement like a Clydesdale. As his arms and legs cut the air, Bernard's shirt ruffled in the wind like the cape of some forlorn superhero.

≈ ≈ ≈ ≈ ≈ ≈ ≈

Sonya Ware decided things were going exactly as they should be. She got the call at work just as she knew she would. The detective delivering the news was vague: *There is a body here, but we're not sure who it is at this time.* Sonya knew the conversation would go like that. Sonya was on her way to the morgue to identify the body, and she was cursing the gang across the street, and this too was as she knew it would be.

She could have written a script for this. In fact, she already had her lines memorized. This nightmare had been played out so many times in her mind, she knew exactly what she would tell the detectives. She knew what she was going to say to her coworkers on the way out of the office. Sonya even knew what she was going to do when she got to the morgue.

She would wail, of course. She would drop to her knees, and someone would try to hold her up, and she would scream,

"That ain't my baby," over and over again. But everyone would know that it was her baby.

Sonya wouldn't be able to rise from the floor at the coroner's office, so the policemen would help her to a seat. And, after an hour with no sign of getting better, they would call an ambulance for her. Sonya would go to the hospital and appear demented as she told the doctors that there was some mistake; that wasn't her baby at the morgue. They would shoot her full of drugs and make her go to sleep, and she would dream about Marcus. Except in her dream her baby would still be alive even though blood was seeping from his head. Marcus would smile and show his mama a somersault.

Sonya waited at a red light on Berry Street and had to put both feet on the brake pedal to keep the car from rolling into the intersection. Her left leg was trembling and had lost most of its strength. The same damned question bounced around Sonya's head, and it wouldn't go away. She slammed her fist on the steering wheel and then slammed her head on it, too, as a distraction. But when the stars faded in the recesses of her mind, the question remained.

Why didn't you move?

But that wasn't fair. She didn't have anywhere to go. She didn't have any money. How was she – no, she stopped herself. This was one part of the script she wanted no part of; the beating herself up on the way to the morgue routine. That had to be the worst reaction, even worse than denying the corpse is her son. Couldn't she hum instead? Couldn't she think of that cute song Marcus used to sing all the time when he got back from Camp Fire?

If all of the raindrops were lemon drops and gum drops...

A blaring car horn startled her. Sonya looked up and saw that the light was green. Apparently it had been for some time. The traffic was moving on both sides of her. The Tahoe behind her was inching closer to her bumper. Why the hell was she alone? Everyone at the office begged to go with her, but she turned them all down. Why?

I need to be alone. I really want to do this by myself.

That was an acceptable answer, but what the hell was she thinking? She shouldn't be by herself at a time like this. Sonya wiped at her face until she could see through her tears. She put her foot on the gas and was moving again. Snot dribbled from her nose and settled on her lips.

"I'd stand outside with my mouth open wide," she whispered. That was always Marcus' favorite part of the Camp Fire song because after that line all of the kids opened their mouths and tilted their heads back and pretended to gobble up gumdrops from heaven.

Another light stopped Sonya at the next intersection. She emitted a violent wail that rattled her bones and shook the frame of her car. It was a dark, guttural sound that was more animal than human. Her baby was gone. She sniffled and wiped her nose. No matter how many times you think something bad is going to happen, life still has a way of catching you off guard. Marcus was going to go to college. All parents say that, but Sonya was sure of it. Marcus had been labeled a "gifted" child since the first grade. He never brought home a report card that he didn't want his mama to see.

"Why, God? Why you take him?" she cried.

Sonya slammed her head on the steering wheel one more time, one *good* time, and when she looked up again she saw them through the gray and black dots swirling behind her eyes. They loitered in the parking lot of a convenience store. There were at least eight of them. Sonya simply could not believe what she was seeing. She stared at them for a long time.

Long tee shirts. Sagging Dickey pants. One of them even had the same afro as the pervert across the street from her house. They were laughing. They were selling drugs right in front of the store as if it was legal. They weren't wearing blue, but they were the same. They were all the same. And they killed her baby.

If all of the snowflakes were chocolate chips and cupcakes...

Another sound ascended from Sonya's gut. It was a wounded sound, but not defenseless. The sound caught in Sonya's throat and began to rattle, and then it became a growl.

When the light turned green this time, Sonya was ready. She slammed her foot hard on the gas pedal, as hard as she could. The sound of screeching tires was melodic to her. She burst through the intersection with burning rubber in her nostrils. She jerked the wheel hard to the right when she got to the corner store, and she jumped the curb with a resounding ***WHUMP!***

The impact with the curb cracked her Chrysler's axle but didn't slow the car much. Sonya plowed into the crowd of gangsters going over 30 miles per hour. As the first body rolled over her hood and smashed into the windshield, Sonya realized that she had seriously deviated from the script. She decided it was worth it.

Oh yeah, totally fucking worth it.

THE DRIVE

Margaret Fowler walked out of the automatic doors and into the brightly lit parking lot of the Super Walmart. It was only a few minutes after seven, but with daylight-savings-time in effect, the auburn sunset had already triggered the store's many fluorescent lights. A few anxious June bugs were flitting about their glow. The August warmth was stifling, even at that late hour. Margaret lived in Overbrook Meadows, a city in central Texas, and there was no relief from the heat expected until early October.

Margaret stepped lightly in beige pumps that matched her beige pants perfectly. She wore a purple blouse that had three large buttons down the middle. She was aware that her outfit lent credence to the suspicion that purple becomes more attractive to women as they age, but if there was a color that complimented beige more than purple, Margaret wasn't aware of it.

She walked casually to her car, unable to shake an unnerving feeling that she had forgotten something. Her shopping list was only four items strong, but she didn't write it down, and her memory was not what it once was. She purchased the correct number of items, but she didn't think one of them had been on her original list. She had the vitamins, that much was obvious because she could hear them rattling in her bag. The coffee definitely wasn't missing. The can of Folgers she bought wasn't the largest, but to Margaret it felt like it weighed fifty pounds.

She shifted her lone bag from one hand to another. The plastic handle immediately squeezed her fresh fingers together as if they were caught in the grip of an uncomfortable handshake. She knew she should have taken her load out in a buggy.

Most shoppers would scoff at the idea of needing a cart to tote one plastic bag, but when you're eighty-nine years old, you really don't give a fart about what people think about you. Margaret didn't give a fart about what her own family thought of her, either, which is why her 1984 Fleetwood Cadillac still hogged the streets of Overbrook Meadows and the parking lot of her favorite store.

Everyone has perceptions about elderly drivers; questions about their possible impairments and the quickness of their reflexes (or lack thereof). But unless you were able to get into the skin of this particular older woman and experience her reflexes for yourself, then nobody – especially not her son – could say what Margaret Fowler was capable of doing.

She promised her son that she would hang up her keys for good on her ninetieth birthday. But that was two years ago, and she didn't believe her abilities declined at all since then. If she was constantly hitting curbs or running cyclists off the road, well that was one thing. But Margaret hadn't been cited for a traffic offense in twenty years. Whether she managed to fit her whole car between the yellow parking lot stripes each time was quite irrelevant, but she did try to park as neatly as possible. Today she didn't do a very good job.

Margaret drove a big car. She loved it. It was big and strong. She wouldn't dream of getting into one of those dainty sedans that were all the rave these days. There was hardly any metal on the frame of those things. Whoever thought it might be a good idea to make a complete front end out of fiberglass may have made a lot of money, but Margaret wouldn't even car pool, let alone drive one of those deathtraps. Her Fleetwood was like something out of a parade, and tonight it looked even longer as it straddled two parking spaces. Nearly the whole front end protruded into the spot to the left of her.

This was the kind of evidence she didn't need. If her son saw this, he would embark on yet another one of his tirades, and Margaret would have to sit there and listen to his nonsensical jabbering: *What if a car had been there? They'd take your license from you then. Do you see how far your nose is in the other guy's space? What if a little kid had been standing there? You could have killed somebody!*

It's odd how parent/child relationships shift over the years. One minute you're wiping boogers from their noses and tying their shoes, but before you know it they're telling *you* what to do.

Margaret was a strong, independent woman. She lived alone; a widow of fifteen years. She paid her own bills and fed herself. The Fleetwood was once her husband's pride and joy. He purchased it brand new in '84 and took excellent care of it until his stroke. Still in pristine condition, the car was now Margaret's most treasured possession. She would stop driving when she was not safe on the roads anymore – she had no objection to that – but *she* would know when that time came. No one had to tell her.

"Open the door and get in the car. Don't look back!"

The voice interrupted her thoughts and Margaret immediately attempted to look over her shoulder. There is something about the words, *Don't look back!* that almost forced you to look back. No one could obey that request, could they?

A hard forearm slammed into the back of her neck coupled with a rough hand gripping the elbow of her left arm. Given Margaret's size and age, the blow to her neck was unnecessarily violent. She stood only 5'1". She had blue eyes and blue hair and more wrinkles than a Shar-pei. No one would consider her a challenge.

Margaret's body lunged forward. The blow was so quick, her head snapped back like someone rear-ended her. Her chest slammed against the Cadillac, whipping her head forward as if on a pendulum. Her chin thumped the driver's door with a resounding *BOMP!* and a dark river of stars swam before her eyes.

Margaret held onto her purse, but her keys and groceries fell from her hands in slow motion. She watched the Folgers' can plummet and bounce free of the bag. It began to roll under the Fleetwood, and in her shock, Margaret cringed at the thought of getting on her knees to retrieve the wayward cylinder. She also remembered what it was she had forgotten to purchase at the store now that her purchases were as scattered as her brain. It was creamer. How had she managed to get the coffee but not creamer? They were on the same aisle.

Standing behind her, the brute kept her pressed against the car with the forearm in her back.

"Open the door," he ordered. His voice was not deep, and there was a slight squeak around the fringes. If not for his obvious strength, Margaret wouldn't have been surprised to turn around and find a teenager assaulting her. But young or old, this was ludicrous. She was old. She weighed no more than 120 pounds. No one attacked little, old ladies anymore. Not in America.

"My ke-. My ke-," Margaret couldn't speak. A sour breath was stuck in her throat, and she couldn't swallow it down. She couldn't breathe. Her heart was like a caged beast in her chest, flapping against her sternum. It would be free. Surely it would break through her paper-thin skin. Her whole body hitched with each heartbeat.

"Open the door!" her assailant ordered again.

Margaret tried to bend to pick up her keys, but her body would not respond. She kicked out a little with her left foot and nudged the keychain. She said, "I dropped them," but it was merely a whisper, and she could barely hear herself over the thunder roaring in her head.

The forearm became a flat palm that pushed into the small of her back. The man stooped behind her and scooped her keys from the pavement. He fidgeted with them for a moment and then asked, "Which one?" He was breathing hard, too.

Margaret stared over the hood of her car. There was another customer making her way out of the sliding double doors, and Margaret thought she saw a uniformed police officer inside the store. Twenty yards away an employee in a blue vest collected runaway shopping carts. Cars were driving here and there. This was senseless. There was going to be witnesses. She was parked under a sign that clearly read, "Smile. You're on Camera." This car thief wasn't going to make it, but still he persisted.

"Which key is it?" he barked into the back of her neck. Margaret cringed from the feel of his breath in her hair. "*Which one?*"

"Take the car," Margaret pleaded. "Just take it. Leave me alone."

"Is it the square one or the round one?"

"It's the square one. With the black rubber on it. Take the car. Let me go back in the store. I didn't see you..."

There was more rustling, and then Margaret heard a dull *click* that was familiar to her. The man moved her back a couple of steps and opened the Cadillac's door. The air was suddenly filled with the scent of violets. The fragrance wafted from a purple palm tree that dangled on her rear-view mirror. Margaret hung the ornament just yesterday. It was fresh, and very strong. Standing in line at 7-11, she thought the aroma was soft and a bit exotic. Now it was pungent. It was foul.

The rough hand moved to her elbow again, pushing her into the car.

"Get in," he muttered.

"Whoa, wha?" This had to be a bad dream. You can always tell when a dream is parading as reality by the nonsensical themes that are produced, like when you're naked at the big presentation, you're falling endlessly, or you're carjacked in broad daylight *and* kidnapped – this was dream stuff.

But at the same time she knew it was all real.

Margaret stood her ground and fought back for the first time. Her son told her many things about emergency situations, but the thing she remembered most was this: *If they are only going to rob you, then they can do that right there. If they want to take you to somewhere, then they have something else in mind.* Even the sickest pervert wouldn't find Margaret's liver-spotted nakedness sexy, so she knew there was only one other thing her assailant wanted her in the car for.

If you know they're going to kill you, then fight right there. Make a scene. They're not going to shoot you in public. Don't go with them. That was the stickler. *Don't go with them.*

Margaret took in a deep breath for what she hoped would be the most horrific shriek since Janet Leigh's shower scene, but her attacker proved to be as primed as he was reckless. From behind, he cupped a hand over her mouth and started shoving her into the car. The Cadillac could easily fit six adults, but Margaret had the front seat pulled up close. Her shoulder banged hard on the steering wheel as she fell forward. The man came in behind her, still pushing.

"Keep going. Move!"

Eventually he had to remove his hand from her mouth, but Margaret didn't react in time. Her scream came out just as he slammed the door closed behind him and effectively muffled the noise. More than the multiple areas of pain raging about her frame, Margaret was aware of her attacker's finesse. He found the lever under the seat, pushed it back to his liking and started her vehicle – all in what she thought was one second.

PLAN C (AND MORE KWB SHORTS)

He yanked the gear-shift into reverse and jerked the steel behemoth out of its parking spot. They exited the parking lot doing a smooth 30, but when they got to the main street, he whipped the wheel to the right with only a minor fishtail. A moment later he was one with the city, traveling a little faster than most but not much more conspicuous than any other vehicle on the road. After two more turns, he felt comfortable enough to slow to the posted speed limits.

≈≈≈≈≈≈≈

It took a great deal of effort, but Margaret was finally able to free her right leg from the uncomfortable position it became trapped in when her body fell upon it. A throbbing, knotting pain radiated from her hip area, and she was pretty sure there was a fracture there, or at least a nasty dislocation. She hadn't heard that dreaded *pop*, but this was a pain she never felt before. Her neck hurt. Her chin was split. Her heart fluttered in her chest.

Margaret had been attacked, kidnapped, and she was now at the will of some creep who obviously meant her harm. But the most pressing fear at that moment was that her heart would fail her. She placed two dainty fingers on her chest as if she could comfort it with her caress.

Margaret kept her head down, but in her peripheral, she could see the scenery blurring at an increased speed. She chanced a peek and saw that they were entering the on-ramp of the city's largest interstate. They were headed south, which didn't surprise her much.

Overbrook Meadows' south side was where most of the city's illicit activities took place. That was where the gangsters did their drivebys, the prostitutes pedaled their stinky wares, and the south was where most of the illegal chemicals that altered your level of awareness were.

Margaret knew her abductor had to be fiending for some kind of narcotics. His crime was idiotic, brazenly stupid. His escape was ill-advised and the victim he selected was unacceptable. They still gave creeps more time for beating up on old ladies, last Margaret heard. If he had any previous criminal history, this offense could get him twenty years easy.

Margaret didn't think he planned on murdering her, because he still didn't want her to see his face. But if she was going to live through the experience, making him pay for this crime was essential. The first step was to identify him. She looked up boldly and caught a swift backhand in return.

"Don't look at me!" he shouted. But the quick glimpse had been enough.

Margaret saw his profile clearly. She closed her eyes, dropped her head, and memorized the smallest details as she rubbed her stinging cheek. Her assailant had thick hair. It was dark and grew past his neckline. There might have been some pattern or hairstyle established, but that had been long ago. His sideburns crept past his earlobe and mingled with a 5 o'clock shadow that was quickly becoming a beard.

His nose was pointed, clearly European, with a distinguishable knot at the bridge. His lips were pursed, but Margaret could tell that they were naturally thin. His beady eyes were not unique, however there was a mole on the corner of his right eyebrow that had sprouted at least one wild hair. He was a skinny guy, no more than 25 years old.

"Gimme your purse," he demanded.

"No," Margaret said defiantly, and she moved the bag away from him, to her right hip. She wasn't an overtly brave woman, but she knew she had to draw the line somewhere. The man wanted her money, not her personal effects. If he wanted her purse, he would have to fight her for it. And, given their high rate of speed, an awesome wreck would surely ensue. Neither of them had on safety belts.

"If you want the money, I'll give it to you," she said, "but you're not digging through my purse with those grubby hands. Beating up on an old lady, you ought to be ashamed of yourself."

Her words were bold, but it was too late to take them back. And it actually felt good to have them out. A warm sensation spread through Margaret's chest and belly. Her husband had told her on more than one occasion that she was, "a tough old bird." It was time to see just how tough she really was. She gripped her purse straps tightly and prepared for the battle. Her attacker hit pretty hard, but had no weapon that she had seen.

"You're not going to give me your purse?" he asked her.

She looked up at him, and said "No."

He looked at her and saw that she was looking at him, but he didn't strike her again. He shook his head and rubbed his eyes. His jaws were sunken, and his wrist was bony. He didn't look like he had the strength to throw her into the Cadillac. Margaret suspected the whole abduction was fueled by adrenaline. Her assailant's next words surprised her but did little to allay the tension.

"Sorry I hit you."

"Well, you should be," Margaret declared, happy they had some type of dialogue going. At least he was capable of remorse. According to her son, talking to an abductor was the best thing a victim could do in situations like this. *Try to make your attacker see you as not just a target, but as a human being.* Margaret was an elderly human being at that.

"How much money you got?" the kidnapper asked, his eyes back on the road. They were still on the interstate, passing exits she was familiar with.

"Well, not a lot," Margaret admitted. "I believe you've wasted your time..." She opened the purse on her lap but kept a tight grip on it lest he attempt to snatch it from her. Her leather wallet was close to the top. If she had any cash, it would be in there. She placed her purse back on her right side and went through the billfold. The punk looked away from the road a lot to make sure she didn't hide anything from him, but Margaret had nothing to hide. There were four one dollar bills, three quarters and six pennies. She removed the currency and placed it on the seat between them.

"This is all I have."

"What about your credit cards?" he asked.

Margaret dug out her bank card and a Master Card. She held them up. "I have these," she said, "but you're not going to be able to use them."

"Why not?" he asked. He wasn't upset by her comment.

"Because the Master Card is almost maxed out, and the bank card won't let you withdraw more than three hundred dollars at a time. I'll have it reported stolen before you make it to the bank." That was another bold move, but Margaret thought she was reading the delinquent pretty well. Whatever he was on was powerful medicine, but it had not taken over his mind to the point where murder might sound like a good idea. He had yet to produce a weapon. This seemed more like a crime of opportunity than a well thought out scheme.

"Where's your bank?" he asked her.

"What do you mean?"

"Your bank. Where is it? We can go right now."

"I told you; you can only get three hundred at a tim—"

"Three hundred's fine," he said. "Where's the bank?"

"Why don't you let me out?" Margaret offered. "I'll give you the pin number. I won't call to report it."

"Sure you won't."

"I promise... You can just, anywhere you want. Pull over right now, and I'll get out, and you'll still have time to go to the bank. There's no way I can get it cancelled that quickly. Just—"

He fixed a stern gaze on her. "Look, lady, I don't want to hurt you. But if you keep jacking around with me, shit's gonna happen. I just want the money, the three hundred or whatever you can get. When I get it, I'll let you go. But if you keep jacking me around, we're gonna have a problem, *see*?"

She didn't *see* anything but a waste of skin and bones.

"You're going to let me go?" she asked.

"I promise. I'll let you go. What do I need you for?"

Resigned to her fate, Margaret exhaled audibly and instructed him to take the next exit and make a u-turn to get to her bank. Her closest bank just happened to be back towards the Walmart, where the police were sure to be canvassing the area.

But the thug said he knew of another First Bank – one not in that direction. He took the next exit and turned right on Seminary Ave.

"You ought to be ashamed of yourself," Margaret reminded him as he veered towards the exit lane.

"I know," he said. "You're right. This shit's crazy."

≈ ≈ ≈ ≈ ≈ ≈ ≈

With money in hand, the kidnapper's mood became noticeably chipper. He smiled as he drove away from the ATM machine.

"So, what now?" Margaret asked him. She had stopped the bleeding from her chin with a handkerchief, but the back of her neck was throbbing with what felt like the first tendrils of a migraine. The pain in her hip had settled into a dull but incessant hum. "Why don't you let me out here?"

The sun was gone now, and Margaret had no desire to see what type of beast her assailant might turn into when the moon rose.

"I have to get something first," he said with a wry smile.

"Well, I don't see why *I* should have to go with you. You've got your money. I don't have anything else to give you." Margaret was pretty sure she didn't have anything else he wanted, but a shudder went up her spine just the same.

He shook his head. "I messed up this time. I really messed it up." Stopped at a light, he looked over at her. She couldn't see much of his expression in the sparse lighting, but he looked genuinely forlorn. "Look, I know you probably don't believe me, but I don't – I didn't want to do this to you."

"Well, I should hope not. But you can make it better," she assured him. "Let me out now. Every moment you keep me, it gets worse."

"Every moment I keep you is all I *got*," he countered. "They don't even know you're missing yet."

"That's impossible," Margaret argued, but she knew it wasn't. She had only seen one patrol car while with her abductor, and that cop didn't show any interest as he passed them at the intersection. If her kidnapper was black, he might have raised more suspicion, but the bastard's white skin kept everything looking normal. Just a grandma out on the town with her grandson. Nothing wrong with that.

"I don't think they're looking for you yet," he went on. "If I let you go, they'll be on my ass as soon as you get to a phone."

There was no arguing that. But this was starting to sound like murder talk again.

"So, what are you going to do with me?" Margaret asked him bluntly. She hadn't made any attempts to jump from the moving vehicle, mainly because of her hip, but she would risk it over an uncertain demise. *Tuck and roll*, she told herself. *It wouldn't hurt that badly.*

"I just wanna get my shit," he said.

Margaret couldn't stop the tears from coming then. She hated herself for it. She wanted to be strong. She felt like she had some measure of control, but the tears belied this. "Don't lie to me!" she spat. "*Just tell me what you're going to do!*"

She watched her abductor's face and saw genuine compassion. He looked into her eyes and winced as if struck.

"Stop that, okay. Just stop... that. I'm not going to hurt you."

"Then let me go!"

"I can't! I told you! I can't! I – I have to get this. If I don't get it, then none of this mattered. And I'm not going through all of this for nothing. If I get caught tonight, I'm going to be high. That's the bottom line. So you're going with me. When I get my shit, you can go. I'm not lying, so, so stop it. Alright? Stop crying. Jeez, you make me..."

Margaret piped down and listened to him. She was a good listener, and she felt like she had a pretty good sixth sense. What he said was miserable and discomforting, but she believed him. The junkie wanted his fix. Margaret wasn't free yet, but a sense of relief fell upon her anyway. She may regret it later, but for now she trusted him. They were headed south again.

After a while Margaret asked, "So, um, what's your drug? What do you do?"

Startled, he asked, "Why do you wanna know?"

"I'm just curious," she admitted. "You beat up an old lady and take her car, I figure it's gotta be something pretty bad..."

He nodded. "What you know about drugs?"

"I know meth is ruining lives nowadays. But crack and heroin are bad, too. I think they're all bad. They make people do stupid things..."

He fixed a hard look on her. "You don't know anything. You know what they say in the paper, and that's it. You don't know what it feels like."

That was true. "What does it feel like?" she asked.

"What is this? A fucking interview?"

"You don't have to use that language with me."

"Well, you don't have to ask me all these questions. Who do you think you are?"

"*You* kidnapped *me*," she reminded him. "I didn't find you. *Hmph.* If you're going to beat me up and rob me, I think I should have some explanation, is all. I think you broke my hip."

"I didn't break your hip. I didn't even touch it."

"Well, when you threw me in the car, I landed on my leg badly." She rubbed the bone for emphasis. "It hurts, and I do believe it's broken."

His face registered sympathy again. "Well, I'm sorry about that."

"You're sorry about a lot of things, young man."

"I don't wanna talk no more," he said, and they didn't.

The thief piloted the Fleetwood to a dark street Margaret had never been on. He turned off the main road onto an even darker avenue. He turned again, and Margaret realized she was essentially lost. She lived in Overbrook Meadows for all 89 years of her life, but she never had cause to visit the neighborhood he took her to.

It was rather shocking to see this part of town, especially after dark. Zombies paced the sidewalks with big eyes and empty bellies. There was a loud argument on one corner, two prostitutes laughing on another. By the time the junkie got to where he was going, Margaret was fearful again. She actually didn't want him to get out of the car to score his dope.

The house they pulled up to was a small, one story shack with bed sheets hung for curtains. There was a porch light on, but no other signs of life. Margaret's kidnapper got out of the car with the keys in hand, and then poked his head back inside.

"If you want, you can leave now."

"Where am I?" she asked.

"You're on the south side. On Jessamine. You've never been here before?"

"No," she said, with wide, frightful eyes.

"If you go west, you'll run into Riverside Drive. You can take Riverside south, back to the freeway."

"I can't walk that far. Take me back to – *somewhere*. Not here. Somewhere brightly lit." She was pleading with him, and that made her angry. "You can't just leave me here! I don't know where I am. I don't know these people."

He smiled. "Well, wait for me, and I'll take you somewhere else."

"Fine, I'll wait," she snapped. "Hurry up!"

It was absurd to negotiate with this bastard, but what choice did she have? Was she going to limp down the street with the zombies? Everyone in this neighborhood was sick and desperate. And Margaret was weak.

≈ ≈ ≈ ≈ ≈ ≈

The thief took the keys with him. In the dark confines of her dead husband's car, Margaret felt more apprehension than she had all night. She had options, but none of them were reasonable.

If she got out of the car, she wouldn't make it too far. She couldn't lock the doors, because her assailant had the keys. Her best bet was to use the cell phone she had in her purse to call the police, but who knew how long it took to purchase drugs?

What if he came back and caught her on the phone? And where would she tell the operator she was? *Somewhere on Jessamine*? She could probably hang up quickly when the junkie came out, but the 911 operator would call her back. Her attacker would know she had been on the phone, and he might not like that.

Nothing seemed like a good idea, so Margaret did nothing and was glad for it. The hoodlum came back to the car within minutes. In one hand he clutched his poison in a death grip. He opened the door and got in quickly.

"You alright?" he asked.

"No. I am *not* alright," Margaret said. "I need to go to the hospital." It didn't take too much acting to make her look pitiful. The contusion on her chin was swollen and purple. She was bruised in more places than she could reach, and her right hip was getting stiff on her.

"We cool now," the kidnapper said. He started the car and backed out of the driveway.

"Where are you going now?" Margaret asked.

"To the park," he said.

"What about me?" A vision of her pale, bloated body stuck in creek weeds flashed before her eyes. "Where are you taking *me*?"

"*I'm* going to the park," he said. "You can get out there. Or you can wait till I'm done, and I'll take you somewhere else."

"You said you were going to let me go."

"You can go," he said. "You coulda got out at that house. You can get out right now." He slowed to a stop, but no one moved. He started driving again.

"I want to go somewhere where I feel safe," Margaret pleaded with him. "Somewhere where there's a phone. And lights."

"There's lights and a phone at the park," he said, but that was a lie.

≈ ≈ ≈ ≈ ≈ ≈ ≈

Sycamore Park was on the corner of Beach and Rosedale Avenue, in the heart of the city's east side. The recreation center closed down two years ago, and it didn't appear that anyone had done any upkeep on the grounds since then.

There were sickly pecan trees, overgrown cycling trails, and the sound and smell of trickling water. There were rusting chain-link fences, unattended trash barrels, and plenty graffiti. But there were no payphones. And the further they drove into that madness, the less lighting there was. The thug finally found a suitable spot amidst the ruins and slowed to a stop.

This is it, Margaret thought. The bastard was going to rape her. But he didn't. He hardly showed any interest in her at all. He reached down and produced an eyeglasses case from one of his socks. The case was old, and it had two thick rubber bands holding it closed.

"How do you turn the inside light on?" he asked Margaret.

"I don't want to see *that*," she told him. "You said you were going to let me go."

"You *can* go," he said and opened the driver's door. The dome light came on, and Margaret could see what she already knew was there. His heroin kit was complete; a small spoon, two needles, a lighter and a bit of cotton.

"There's no light here," Margaret said. "You said there were lights here. And there's no phone. How am I supposed to call for help?"

But the addict was busy now. He didn't look up from his work. "There's enough light for you to see. Just go up that way." He nodded towards a spooky trail. "It'll take you back to Rosedale."

42

"*I can't walk,*" she reminded him.

"Then wait a minute," he said. "I'll take you."

That was the last straw. Margaret let out a loud *HMPH!* – a sound only pissed off grandma's can make – and she opened her door.

He looked up at her. "What are you doing?"

"You said I could go, right?"

"I thought you couldn't walk."

"Well, I'm not going to sit here and watch you do *that*. If I can't walk, I'll crawl. But come hell or high water, I'm getting out of this car this very minute."

He smiled. "Okay, go." He had the dope in the spoon now.

Margaret scanned the darkened park and then looked back at her abductor. She decided she was screwed either way. She took a deep breath and clenched her teeth together. She knew it was going to hurt, but no amount of preparation readied her for the pain she felt when she put weight on her right hip.

"*Oww! Oooh!*" She let out a deep howl and fell back into the seat. Her hip was broken. There was no doubt about it. She gritted her teeth and took a few hurried breaths. Beads of sweat blossomed on her face and neck.

"You alright?"

She turned and fixed a look of disgust on the man. "*You broke my hip!*" she bawled.

"It's alright," he said. "I'll take you to the doctor in just a minute." He had the fire going under the spoon, and the car started to smell like dope.

Margaret wanted to cry out, but she used her last bit of strength to maintain her composure. They waited in silence for a few heartbeats. She watched the spoon, the man's face, and then the spoon again. She didn't know what type of animal her attacker would become once he put that needle in his arm, and she had no intentions of finding out.

"Are you a religious man?" she asked him.

He didn't look up. "I don't know."

"I have this prayer card," she said, digging in her purse. "There's a prayer here... I want to read it to you. Here it is."

By the time he looked up, the gun was in her hand. It was a dark-colored piece, a .38 Special to be precise. It was a revolver, so he knew she didn't need to cock it.

Margaret pulled the hammer back anyway.

"This is my husband's car," she said calmly. "Get out." That was an order, and it felt good to give an order after being at the thug's mercy for so long. It felt so good she said it again. "*Get out!*"

Margaret's heart wasn't worn out after all. It kicked like a bass drum now.

The creep moved. Maybe he was moving towards her. Maybe he was going to get out as she instructed. Who's to say?

Margaret squeezed the trigger.

BLAK!

The gun jumped in her hand. The explosion was deafening in the confines of the Cadillac. The round hit him on his right side, sending blood and smoke spitting out of a fresh hole on his other side. The junkie dropped his lighter and his fix. He barely had time to register a look of shock before Margaret pulled the trigger again,

BLAK!

catching him higher in the chest this time. With her ears still ringing, she thought the second shot would be less earsplitting, but it wasn't.

The impact was like a kick from a mule. The junkie's sternum cracked and folded in on itself. He let out a startled "*Waaah?*" and his beady eyes grew to cartoonish proportions.

The look on his face was priceless. Margaret didn't want to take any pleasure in this, but that look – she couldn't have planned it better if she was directing a movie. He was dumbfounded. Incredulous. You could read the expression on his face: *How could she? How could she shoot me? She wasn't supposed to have a gun. She was weak. Defenseless. She's... killing me...*

And that she was.

Margaret sat there under the soft glow of the Fleetwood's dome lights and watched him die. She did not attempt to get out of the car again. She didn't immediately go for her phone. She sat and watched him.

Her attacker coughed. He gargled the blood in his lungs and spat some of it out. He pawed at his wounds. His heart pumped blood out of the hole in his chest and out of his mouth and nose as well. It spilled down his belly in frothy streams. After what felt like an eternity, he vacated his bowels and then leaned towards the open driver's door. He fell halfway out of the car but didn't take his odors with him.

Margaret sat calmly with her gun still trained on him and watched the whole thing. When he finally stopped moving and she was sure he was dead, she returned the pistol to her purse and fished out the cell phone. Her ears were still ringing. The two gunshots reverberated in her memory and would continue to do so for years to come.

Margaret called her son before she called 911. Pete was a police officer. He was familiar with the area and promised to be there in ten minutes. Pete wanted her to stay on the phone with him until he got there, but Margaret assured him the junkie was one hundred percent dead. Pete then told her to hang up with him and call 911. He wanted her to call him back after she talked to the operator, but he knew they would want her to remain on the line with them.

Margaret disconnected with her son and dialed the three emergency numbers. Before she pressed send, a voice spoke up in the back of her mind. It was a weak, timid voice: *You just murdered a man, Margie. You killed him in cold blood. You were armed, and he wasn't and he was going to get out of the car. You know he was going to get out of the car.*

She sneered and shut that voice up quickly. That was hogwash. No one in the world would prosecute a little, old lady who defended herself against a violent drug addict. Her son gave her the gun for protection. And if ever there was a situation to use it, this most certainly was it. They might give her a medal, but she wouldn't have to defend her actions to anyone, not even herself.

What about God? the voice wanted to know. *He knows what you did.*

Margaret was a little put off then. This was ridiculous. Here she was, battered and bruised with a dead guy bleeding in her late husband's car. How screwed up in the head was she that she was blaming herself for this? She told the scary, little voice to go to hell.

Whether the junkie was getting out of the car or coming at her, Margaret did what had to be done. The addict could have done this again one day. And what if it wasn't an old lady, but a young mother next time? Lord knows what he might have done to a pretty, young girl in this park. No. If ever there was an event to chalk up to *Good Riddance*, this was definitely it.

"Good riddance," Margaret whispered into the awful darkness, and that sounded like a pretty good ending to her.

STABLER

"Hello? Is somebody there?" He yelled this knowing full well I was there, and then he coughed. It was a sick, dry cough. I already had a sneer on my face due to the smell, but I wrinkled my nose a little more in disgust. He didn't sound too good. He sounded like he needed a tall glass of water. A burger would be good too, but water should come first. Actually, if you want to get technical about it, Gatorade would be more appropriate at this point, because I hadn't given him any fluids in two days. I knew he was okay, though. I wasn't going at this blind. I did plenty of research. I knew he could go three to five days without water before succumbing to death.

From what I've read, dehydration is a pretty good way to die. There are lots of tantalizing stages: First comes the extreme thirst, of course. You get the worst case of dry mouth *ever*, and your saliva becomes thick and frothy. After a few days, you become dizzy, disoriented, and even standing is too much of a chore. Sitting isn't much of a picnic either, which is why most of the starving Africans on those long, sad infomercials are lying on their backs. Speaking of those commercials, dehydration also leads to *gastroenteritis*, which is why their bellies swell to the size of plump watermelons. I don't know about you, but I've always wondered about that.

Anyway, as dehydration progresses, there is a good deal of agony. Your muscles cramp in the arms and legs, and you're hurting so much you would cry if you could, but as you might expect, your body isn't going to waste any moisture on tears. Your stomach cramps, your skin dries out and cracks, and your hands and feet get cold because any of your body's remaining fluids are diverted inward, towards your vital organs. By day four or five, your brain begins to shrink, which causes hallucinations and seizures. Finally, your blood pressure drops to almost undetectable levels, and your heart has a major arrhythmia. This is when the sweet angel of death becomes your best friend.

I researched dehydration because this is the fate I initially wanted for Stabler. If you're a *Law and Order* fan, you'll want to pronounce it St*a*bler, with a short "*a*" sound, like in the word "stay." Although this is actually the correct pronunciation according to his lineage, I, as well as the rest of the world, know this guy as *Stabler;* pronounced with a flat "*a*," like in the word "stab."

I believe it was a local reporter who first gave him the nickname. It stuck and was embraced by all because Stabler had a propensity to *stab* people. The media had a field day with this. Tabloids nicknamed him *The Stabler*, or *Mr. Stabler the Murder Man*, but we'll get to that later.

After my readings, I wanted Stabler to die of dehydration. From what I read, that seemed like an excellent way to go. And as I thought back on the looks of woe on those dark faces in the commercials, I started visualizing Stabler with that same look. I would lie awake at night and fantasize about him with big, skeleton-style teeth poking past thin lips. Sunken cheeks and hollow eye sockets with bulging, glistening eyeballs that attracted flies. Skin stretched taut over his skull.

Ten years ago, visions like that at bedtime would have had me tossing and turning like any normal person. But after the trial, thoughts of Stabler's slow demise were smile-inducing.

Gradually and reluctantly I had to decide against dehydration because it wasn't something I could totally control or trust. I knew I wasn't going to take him to my house – that's the first place they'd look – and I wouldn't be able to make a lot of trips to this alternate location to check on his progress, either. I had Stabler in a deserted area, miles away from civilization. I had no fear of him escaping, but anything could happen. If *I* found the place, someone else could also. No matter how improbable it was that someone would happen upon my spot after half a century of idleness, I couldn't rule it out one hundred percent.

Also rumor had it there were wild dogs in the region. Don't get me wrong, Stabler being eaten alive by ravenous mouths would be wonderfully gruesome, but with my luck the canines might rip out his throat right away. That's the way wild beasts do it on the National Geographic channel. I wanted Stabler's suffering to be anything but brief, which is why I decided to do it myself.

There's no substitute for ones' own warped diligence.

I dropped my bag and tools noisily on the concrete floor because it was okay to let him know I was back. I wanted him to know that I was very close and that I had clinking metal instruments with me. This wait was a form of psychological torture, and it would be the kindest torture Stabler was apt to receive from me.

I knew I would get a response. I had him for a couple of days already, and I didn't check on him at all during this time. Every time I made noises, he went to jabbering.

"Hello? Hello? Is someone there?" He waited for a while and then said, "Hey, I don't know what I did to you – why you're doing this to me – but *I'm sorry*. Okay. Just let me go. I won't tell. Nobody has to know."

Stabler had to know that he wasn't going to make it out of this alive. Surely he knew his abductor was a psychopath. Anyone who would go through all the trouble of breaking into his home while he slept, binding and drugging him, and then driving him to an undisclosed location some 800 miles away wasn't going to simply let him go.

Stabler wasn't able to see any street signs or landmarks during our trip, but he was awake for most of the ride. He *felt* it. And Stabler was a smart man. As a matter of fact, he scored near genius-level on his I.Q. tests. He knew he was far from home, and he was most certainly fucked. Yet he begged anyway.

The begging gave me pleasure, though, so I listened intently. I had a tape recorder with me. I knelt and unzipped my duffle bag slowly and rummaged through its contents for the device. I did everything slowly and deliberately. Every sound was necessary for the performance. And if I played my cards right, this would be the performance of a lifetime.

"Hey, why don't you come and talk to me. We can talk about this. These ropes are tight. Chains? Straps? I'm not going to get away. C'mon, man, let's talk."

"*I'm coming,*" I crooned in his direction. I thought he would recognize my voice, but he didn't.

"Good. That's good, man. We can talk. Who are you? Why are you doing this to me?" I heard muffled rattles as he jerked against his restraints, but he was right about one thing: He wasn't going to get away.

"I said '*I'm coming!*'" I barked. Stabler was used to getting his way, but this was going to be a reckoning. No jury, no judge, and no shiesty lawyer was here to help him now. I stood and stuffed the tape recorder into my back pocket, and then I marched purposefully in his direction. We were only separated by one wall. I only had to round the corner to see how the hours had been treating him. I couldn't have asked for better.

Benjamin Stabler sat just as I had left him, except for the dark rings under his bloodshot eyes and a dark stain in the crotch of his khaki pants from either a defecation or urination accident. The chair I bought for him was perfect. Called an *extraction chair*, it was used mainly in hospitals, but law enforcement agencies were also making use of them nowadays. Brand new, the chair costs up to a thousand dollars. But I managed to find a used one for almost half that. Similar to a dental chair, I could raise it up, extend the legs and recline it until the subject's feet were completely off the ground. That last one is the position I had it in for Stabler.

The chair came with straps for every limb and a harness for the torso. There was even a restraint for the head, but I upgraded it with a few more ropes and chains of my own. Unless he could turn big and green and burst through his clothing, there was no way Stabler was getting out of that chair. The only thing I didn't like about it was the padding included for the patient's comfort, but this is one luxury I would allow.

As I stepped into the room, Stabler's face registered foggy recognition. I flashed a hearty smile and said, *"Yeah, it's me!"*

We met dozens of times during his trial. Well, I can't say we had a formal *How do you do*, but we would have if he had been found guilty. I already had my speech planned for the sentencing phase when I, the victim, would be allowed to confront the accused. The sentencing phase never came up, but I still felt like I knew Stabler personally. I read every article ever written about him, I never missed a day in court, and after the trial I studied the case records as if I was cramming for the BAR.

Stabler's current appearance was a far cry from the clean-cut professional he portrayed at the courthouse two years ago. In just forty-eight hours, he already looked like he'd been interrogated by the KGB. His dirty-blonde hair was disheveled. His blue eyes, once confident and striking, were weak and pained.

He wore a maroon cardigan with khaki pants and nothing else. This was an outfit he probably wouldn't dream of wearing under normal circumstances, but I dressed him myself, and I wasn't too particular about what I put on him. When I broke into his home, I was disgusted to find that he slept in the nude. But clothing him only took a few minutes. I still left his property within the time block I'd allotted for the abduction.

Stabler didn't have much mobility, but I saw his whole body tense.

"You're right," I said. "Those straps are a little too tight. Your left hand is almost purple. Can you move your fingers?" His eyes didn't leave my face. Those baby blues scanned my features, but I didn't think he was going to get it. I know I looked different, too. I'd lost nearly forty pounds in the two years since the trial. I had also been wearing my hair very short in the past year in preparation for this. Today I wore a gray jogging suit with white socks and shoes that were two sizes too big. I purchased each article of my outfit at three different locations. Stabler had never seen me in anything but a suit.

"Come on," I said. "I know you can't remember *every face*, but you know mine."

His bottom lip quavered, and he tried to shake his head.

"You want me to loosen that for you?" I asked as I approached him. "I can take that strap off your head if you want. A man should be able to move his head. You've probably got one hell of a cramp – *Eww!* What's that *smell*?"

I stopped short and gave him a look of repulsion. "That's *nasty*, man. If you had to go to the bathroom, you should have said something."

He didn't respond.

I shook my head and continued towards the back of the chair. I wore blue latex gloves under my leather ones. Combined, they were hot and uncomfortable, but this was something I could easily endure. I continued to berate him as I undid the strap.

"You're not a child anymore, Benjamin. You're a grown man. You're too big to be pissing on yourself. And you're definitely too big to do number *two* in your pants. I don't know what I'm going to do with you..." Finished with the strap, I went back around to face him. "That better?"

Stabler couldn't take his eyes off of me. He popped a couple of kinks out of his neck. His eyes remained fixed on mine.

"You're Barrett," he said finally.

I couldn't hide my elation. "Good. *Good*! Now, where do you know me from?"

His chest started to rise and fall noticeably. "Look, man, I didn't do it. They let me go. I got acquitted*!* I didn't do it. I swear I didn't do it."

I gave him a big frown and held up one finger. I waved it slowly as if he was a naughty boy. "No, no, no. See, that won't do. I'm sorry. This is my fault. I should have explained the rules first. I only have a few. The first rule is you have to respond directly to my questions. The second rule is you can't lie about anything. Look around." I waved my arm to encompass the room.

There were only gray, concrete walls and gray concrete floors. A lone window was built into the wall behind me, but it wasn't the type that would open. It was our only source of light. It was early morning, and I hoped to be done with him by nightfall. But I brought a generator and lamps just in case. Besides Stabler's seat, the only other furniture in the room was a metal folding chair leaning against a far wall. There was plenty dust, even more cobwebs, but nothing extraordinary. The room had the feel of a place that had not been inhabited in quite a while.

"There's no one here," I said. "No judge, no lawyer, no cameras. You don't have to worry about any of that anymore. All you have is me, and I–"

"C'mon, man. You can't do–"

I surged forward and delivered a vicious backhand across his face. I hit him hard. There was seven years of hate in that slap. Seven years of pain. Seven *long* years. The sharp **SMACK!** reverberated around the room for a few seconds. Stabler's head snapped to the side hard enough to cause whiplash, and he yelped like a frightened puppy.

"*Whay, wait!* What are you doing? Stop, man. *Stop!*"

The natural reaction to someone hitting you is to raise your hands in defense. Stabler tried, but couldn't. That must have been a dreadful feeling.

I stepped back like a disciplined soldier. "Oh, I'm sorry, Benji. I forgot to tell you another one of my rules."

"*What*?" he cried.

"You do not interrupt me while I am speaking," I said. "That's just rude."

"*I didn't do it*," he bawled. Nearly the whole side of his face was turning a bright, fire hydrant red. A little blood trickled out of the corner of his mouth. "*I didn't do it! You were there! You heard them! I got out free, man. They let me go!*"

"That's right, Mr. Murder. They let you go. That's why *I* have you. Do you know where you are?"

Stabler looked around frantically. He jerked at his restraints, but I'm sure he'd been jerking at them all night with no luck. "Listen, man," he reasoned. "I got money. They want to do a book and a movie. I can–"

I stepped forward quickly and delivered another open-handed blow.

SPLACK!

"*Wha-*"

I stepped back to my position. "You will respond to the question asked, Benjamin. You're a smart man. This shouldn't be that hard for you."

"You didn't say that was a rule!"

"Oh, I didn't? Hmm. Okay, well I owe you one." I smiled. "When you get out, I'll let you hit me *one* time. Deal?"

"When are you going to let me go?"

I chuckled. "See, technically, that's another slap for you. I know I'm splitting hairs here, but when I said, '*Deal*?' that was a question. Your lack of response means it's time for another slap, right? These are the rules we both agreed on. So now we're even."

"I didn't agree to any rules! Man, you gotta be out of your mind." He looked around at the walls and his restraints. "There's no way you're going to get away with this. Absolutely no way. This is *2013*. You can't do this stuff nowadays." He thought for a moment. "*Did you come to my house?*"

"Of course I went to your house. How do you think you got here?"

"Someone helped you?"

I shook my head. "No, Stabler. No one helped me. You only weigh about one-eighty. I got fifty pounds on you. And with my adrenaline pumping, you were like a big sack of potatoes. I dropped you once in the driveway, though. But you were out, man. Feeling no pain."

"What'd you drug me with?"

"Chloroform. Also known as trichloromethane."

"How'd you get that?"

"On the internet," I said. "You can get anything on the internet. I found your chair on the internet. Good thing about the internet is they don't care who's buying what, as long as you have a credit card number."

"So you ordered all this stuff on your credit card?"

"Stabby, come on, man. Give me some credit. You can go to any Ace check cashing place and get a pre-paid Visa. You can put however much you want on it. It's not really a credit card, though. You can't get anything *on credit*. But you can use it on the internet like a credit card."

"Where are we?" he asked.

"*Geez*. So many questions. Oh, I get it." I grinned at him. "We're going to do the Batman thing, right? I'm the evil villain, and you're the superhero; tied up with no possibility of escape, right? I'm supposed to reveal all of my fiendish plans so you can thwart them when you get away, huh? Okay, let's do that. I've always wanted to do that.

"Yes, Mr. Stabler, I broke into your house. I wanted to get you every since they let you walk out of that courtroom, but I knew I couldn't do anything right away. I mean, I *was* on Oprah after all, crying and cursing your very existence and such. So of course I couldn't kidnap you then. I waited. And you know what? After a while the tabloids stopped calling, and the reporters stopped following me around.

"I knew it would take a little longer for you, though. You know, 'cause you're Mr. Murder. But I waited and waited and, well, this is gonna sound creepy, but I started following you again six months ago. I moved pretty close to you. You didn't seem too cautious anymore. As a matter of fact, you started to look downright complacent. You moved out of that condo with the good security guard. What was his name? Gary? You know, the fat guy with those rolls of meat on the back of his neck that looked like sausages... Anyway, you moved into that house, and I'm thinking, '*Does he think he's just going to live happily ever after?*'

"Is that what you thought? Well, I hope you've learned a lesson here. You let your guard down, and now you're *not* happily ever after. You know, I think I got you right in time. That new one you've been following around, the one from South Hills Elementary, you were going to take her, weren't you? You're about due for another one, aren't you? You're sick, man. That girl's like, nine years old. *Nine years old.*

"Do you know what they would have done to you in the joint? *Low Eyes* – that's what they'd call you. They'd make you hold their pants as they walked around the yard. Seriously. I heard that in prison they make their *bitch*, that'd be you, hold the front of their pants. You know, where a belt buckle would be. They'd walk around, and you'd have to follow them, holding their pants so everyone would know you're that guy's property.

"That would have been good for you, but I think this is cool, too. You're in an abandoned pickle factory in Texas. That's right, Benji, *a pickle factory*, and yes, I did say *Texas*. According to your bio, you've never been to Texas. That's sad. It's only three states away. You really should get out more. Beautiful state. Everything's big here, just like they say.

"This is the McBain Pickle Factory. They call it a factory, but by today's standards, it really doesn't measure up. It's barely bigger than your house. Ever heard of McBain Pickles? No? Me neither. They went belly up in 1943. I mean, who's gonna want a *McBain* pickle when they can have a Best Maid or Vlasic?

"McBain never was too big time to begin with. There's not even an interstate or major road that passes this place. They had dirt roads back then, and the ones around here aren't in use anymore. You should see this place from the outside. Can't hardly tell it's here because of the trees and shrubs.

"I've heard that nature will take back a whole town, even one as big as New York City, if us humans left it alone for like, 50 years or so. That's what it looks like here. Nothing but trees 'til you get really close.

"Anyway, that's my spiel. Any more questions?"

Stabler looked away from me for the first time. "What happened to my dick?"

"What do you mean?" I said, then, "*Oh*, you're talking about – hey, man, I'm no pervert. Let's get that straight right now. *You're the freak.* I'm just disgruntled. When I put your pants on, the little booger got caught in the zipper a couple of times. My bad. But it's all good. Nothing major. A little ointment, and you'll be back to raping in no time."

"You're not going to get away with this," he promised.

I shook my head. "Now that's odd coming from you. You got away with murder – four times that we know of. You are Mr. Murder. If anyone knows that you can indeed get away with stuff like this, it should be you."

"I didn't kill anyone," he contended. "And you, you probably left fingerprints all over my house."

I held up my gloved hands and smiled.

"Mr. Barrett," he said, "you know that's not gonna do it. You still got hair, skin... Your DNA's all over the place."

"No, I don't think so, Stabler. I had on a full thermal. Over that I wore a jumpsuit, sorta like the one I have on now. I had a ski mask on, too. They might find a few threads from the jump suit or the mask, but they're cheap and sold everywhere.

"The only way they can match any fibers from that outfit to me, is if I still have the outfit in my house when they come to question me, which I won't. I have those clothes in the trunk of the car out there. And I plan on burning it thoroughly. I even wore shoes that were two sizes too big in case they found fresh footprints in the morning dew."

"Your car," Stabler said, sure he had me. "Tire tracks, neighbors..." His lip was starting to swell, and he was developing a lisp. "No way you drove all the way to Texas without someone seeing you."

"Alright, you got me." I held my hands up in surrender. "It's not my car. I had to steal it. I know; I'm a terrible person. If they trace the car, it'll come back stolen. And by the time they find it, it'll be all burnt up. It's pretty hard to get evidence from a burnt car, Benji. I looked into it. CSI hates it when you burn a car. Not the TV CSI, but the *real* CSI. They hate burnt cars."

Rather than more fearful, Stabler appeared to become more smug: "So you think you got it all figured out, huh? Covered all your bases?"

"Well, let's see. You killed six little girls, my daughter included. They found items from my daughter's purse at your home." I caught a hitch in my throat, and that pissed me off. I wanted to be strong with this. "They found a couple of Amy

Winslet's hairs in your vehicle. Witnesses saw you walking out of the mall with Tabitha Cage, and a traffic camera has a picture of you in the car with a little girl who looked a lot like Samantha Pierce. Not to mention your confession to the murder of Amy. But you still managed to beat it, didn't you? You beat all of that, but I can't pull off one kidnapping? Come on, Ben. I'm not a stupid man."

"That confession was thrown out! Inadmissible in court!"

"They have it on video," I reminded. "You can try to take it back all you want, but they have a video tape. You remember when Clinton said, *'I did not have sexual relations with that woman?'* Hard to take it back when you can rewind the tape."

"It was thrown out! And anybody could have been in the car with me that day. I saw that picture. You can't say that was her. And I never walked out of the mall with Tabitha Cage! They never found anything at my house, either. That *so-called* evidence was thrown out, too. Nobody followed protocol on that search. By the time they got through, everything was completely tainted. First they said they found that girl's hair in my house, and then they said it was in my car. You can't trust any of that. They could have gotten it from anywhere."

"But they did get *something* from your home, Stabler. Detective Rick Murphy stated that on the morning of July 12, 2007, he recovered my daughter's bracelet and earrings from your home." My heart hitched again.

"He could have got that stuff from anywhere!"

"He says he got it from your home!" I wanted to stay calm, but my daughter's belongings were found at this creeps house. To this very day, it is still considered evidence. I can't have it back, but for three years this guy had it.

"If he got it from my house," Stabler said, "then he should have done his paperwork correctly, and we wouldn't be here today! That was the weakest link anyway. That's circumstantial. They can't say I killed someone just by planting a couple of trinkets in my house."

"Circumstantial?" I asked him. I don't know how I was maintaining my composure, but I was. "Hmm. Well, let's talk about what we know for sure. We know who killed Lacy Rivers, don't we?" I dug deep for this one.

"I was twelve years old. That has not–"

"Twelve years old, right. And they didn't know you did it at first. She was your next door neighbor. Puberty came a little early for you, huh? And you almost got away with it. What messed you up? Oh yeah. I remember. A year and a half later you got that itch again, didn't you? You remember Trisha Yarborough? Sexually assaulted and stabbed, just like Lacy. They put it together then, didn't they?"

"That was twenty years ago! I did my time!"

"Of course you did. For those two murders, you lived in the mental wing of a state hospital, playing stupid for eight years. *Eight years*. Some idiot judge released you on your twenty-first birthday. You promised to be a good little boy, and you've been a model citizen since then, huh? Everything is circumstantial and coincidental since then, right? You admit to the first two–"

"I was a kid!"

I drew back to deliver a blow, but didn't. *"No interrupting,"* I warned. "You'll admit to the first two. You were just a kid. You served your time. But you won't take any responsibility for the last four although circumstantial evidence puts you around them or their property around you. The last four were molested and stabbed in a manner similar to the first two, is that right?"

"No, that's not right," he said. "I mean, I don't know about the last four. I don't know how they were stabbed or whatever happened to them."

"Well, I do. They were all picked up in public places, which is your M.O. They were all driven to a location, which was most likely *not* your home. And they were all sexually assaulted by someone who wore a condom. They were all stabbed multiple times, always in both breasts and *always* in the neck. Lacy and Trisha's twenty year old crime scenes look just like the four new ones, but that's all circumstantial, right?"

"It wasn't enough!" The muscles in his neck bulged. "You know it wasn't me! You sat in that court room everyday, just like I did. You heard the testimony."

"Yeah, I heard your lawyer tell the judge that just because you killed these other two girls twenty years ago, didn't mean you had anything to do with these other four."

"Right."

"And just because you were seen in a vehicle with a little girl who resembled Samantha Pierce didn't mean you took her somewhere and molested her."

"I didn't."

"And just because you were at the mall with Tabitha didn't mean you killed her, either."

No response.

"And just because they found my daughter's bracelet and earrings on your bathroom counter didn't mean you molested my little girl either, right?" My eye twitched this time. I wanted to choke him to death more than I wanted my next breath, but I resisted. He was right. So far this *was* all circumstantial.

"They didn't find it at my house." He was more subdued now.

"Where did they find it?"

"I don't know."

"They found it somewhere."

"The whole case was circumstantial."

"I know, Stabler. I know."

"Stop calling me that! My name is Stabler!"

I ignored him. "You can't build a case on circumstantial evidence, Mr. Murder. The district attorney tried, and we saw how that turned out. Which leads to why we're here."

Stabler looked around. "What do you want? If you're going to kill me, just do it."

"If I wanted to kill you, I could have done so at your home," I told him. "Do you know how much chloroform it takes to kill a man your size? Not a lot. I don't want you dead, killer. I want what any rational individual wants: I want a confession." I pulled the tape recorder from my pocket.

He looked at it for a moment and then smiled. He shook his head. "That ain't gonna work. This is *duress*. No judge would take that. You're crazy, Barrett."

"Oh, I don't want it for a judge, Ben. I want it for *me*. I mean, if there's even the *slightest* chance I got it wrong... Me and the whole world, everyone's got it wrong. If you're innocent, I just wouldn't feel right about myself, you know?"

Stabler shook his head and grinned at me. "Man, you're some piece of work. You want me to confess to crimes I did not commit so you'll feel better about your kidnapping, assault and

I'm sure there's some law against drugging me, too – and whatever else you've done.

"You're not getting a confession out of me. I'm innocent. I'm sorry for what happened to your daughter, but you're not pinning that on me. They tried, I beat it, and that's it. If you let me go right now, I'll forget this ever happened. I'll even get my own ride home. You can still make it right, buddy. You don't want this on your conscious."

I nodded. "Alright, Stabber. I guess I have to up the ante." I turned and walked out with him still grinning.

"Where you going?" he called after me.

"To get my bag," I said.

My bag was nothing special; a standard green and black gym bag. It didn't even have a logo. When I rounded the corner on the way back to him, his smug expression was gone. I sat the bag down in front of him and then turned my back to get the folding chair. When I faced him again, he was trying to get a look at the bag, but he couldn't see it past his own feet. I sat with the bag on the floor between us.

"Man, you really stink," I said as I unzipped the gym bag. "I mean, I've smelled some raunchy things in my time, but you should be ashamed of yourself. It's only been two days, Stabby. You could have held it."

"What are you gonna do?" he asked.

"I'm going to do *different things* with *different things*," I told him. Since he couldn't see what I had, I held the items up individually.

"*These*," I said, showing him my first toy, "are artery forceps. I like 'em 'cause you can clamp down on something, and they'll lock with that pressure. You don't have to hold it yourself. I have six of these. I'm going to clamp them on various parts of your body, come back later and clamp them on six different parts."

He didn't like the looks of those forceps. I held up something he liked less.

"This is a Bowman speculum." I squeezed the handles. "Eye doctors use it to hold eyelids open during surgery. I was thinking about propping yours open for a little of this..." I held up a small container the size of a glue bottle. "This is bleach." I peered down into my bag. "I also have some lemon juice, concentrated chlorine, hydrochloric acid, sulfuric acid. I like your blue eyes. I'm obsessed with them really, so I also have this…" I showed him a small, pointy instrument. "This is a cataract knife. I know you don't have cataracts, but eye surgery has always been interesting to me."

His eyes were huge, but he didn't respond, so I kept going.

"These are nasal cutting forceps."

"This is a Heister's mouth gag."

"Biopsy forceps."

"Scalpel. Scalpel. More scalpels. Wow. I didn't think I had this many…"

"Bone saw."

"Plaster saw."

"Splinter forceps."

"Rib shears, lobectomy scissors, and… Yeah, that's it." Still peering into the bag, I said, "I've got plenty salt for your wounds. I have these…" I held up a large mason jar. "I read some reports from that hospital you were in when you were a kid. Supposedly you're afraid of spiders. You still afraid of spiders?"

The tarantulas were huge but harmless. Totally domesticated, you could squeeze one half to death before it would bite, but Stabler didn't know that. He gasped and farted at the same time.

I returned the jar back to the bag, and he strained his neck trying to keep track of them.

I waved a hand in front of my face. "Goodness, man. If you're going to be farting, try to warn me next time. *Jeez.*" I rummaged through the bag a bit more.

"Well, that's pretty much it. I've got duct tape, vice-grips, a lead pipe, Vaseline… You know, the basics. Oh, and this." I lifted a brand new pair of pliers. "These are old-school, I know, but I like 'em." Finally, I removed a manila envelope from the bag and placed it on my lap. "You ready?"

"What do you want me to do?" he asked. He was scared and couldn't hide it anymore. I think it was the spiders that got him.

I removed a photo from the envelope. It was large, 8 by 11 inches, so I didn't have to hold it too close. I showed him the picture. "This is Lacy Rivers, your first victim."

He barely glanced at the black and white photo.

"Did you kill her?" I asked.

"You know I killed her," he said, no longer raising his voice.

"Oh, hold on." I put the picture down and found my tape recorder. I set it to record and then placed it on his chest. "Alright. Now."

He shook his head. "I'm not doing that."

I nodded and went back into my bag. "Oh yeah, I have one more thing here." I removed a leather shoulder holster and stood to strap it on. I then produced a chrome .45 automatic. "This is a nice gun," I said. "Brand new. Never fired. It's going to be loud as hell in here."

He stiffened but didn't panic. "If you're going to kill me, just do it now."

I nodded. I cocked the gun and pointed it at his face. He winced.

"If you want me to kill you, I will. But I don't have to. I told you, I just want your confessions."

"You're going to kill me anyway."

"Why would I do that?" I asked. "If I kill you, you get off easy. I want you in prison for the rest of your life. I don't even want the death penalty. I want you holding that big guy's britches, taking that big guy's dick for twenty or thirty years."

"It's not gonna work. They'll throw it out. This is duress."

"So what difference does it make to you?" I asked. "If they throw it out, then you get off again. What's the problem?" I still had the gun trained on him.

"They'll lock you up. You know it."

"Lock me up for what? Kidnapping the murderer of my daughter and forcing him to confess? Shit, I'm under duress, too. I'm clearly off my rocker. Maybe I can get a cushy mental hospital deal like you did."

He thought it over for a minute. "It's not gonna work. They'll throw it out."

"That's up to them," I said.

He waited another minute and then said what I'd been waiting to hear.

"You're going to let me go?"

I leaned towards the recorder and said, "I'm going to let you go."

"Alright," he said finally. "I killed her."

I smiled and un-cocked the weapon. I slid it into my holster and sat down. I held the picture up again. "How did you kill her?" He stared at me and knotted his eyebrows, breathing fire through his nostrils. I waited a while and asked again. "How did you kill her?"

"I stabbed her," he said finally.

"Good," I said. "But I want you to go back a little. Go back to the abduction."

"What?"

"How did she get from sleeping in her bed one night to being dead the next night? Tell me how you abducted her."

"This is already prosecuted. Why do you need it? It's in the records. I did my time."

"That's why I don't see what the big deal is," I said.

"She was my friend," he said.

I listened. The tape recorder hummed.

"We played together sometimes. There was a vacant house in our neighborhood, about a quarter mile from where we lived. It had been vacant for over a year, but there was still furniture in there. A lot of junk in the garage. We used to go to the garage to play sometimes, looking for old stuff."

I nodded. Lacy's body was found in a vacant garage close to her home. This was all in the records.

"Did you take the knife with you?"

He snarled but kept talking. "I took it there two days before. I tried to get her there a couple of times, but she couldn't go. When we got there the third day, I killed her."

"How did you kill her?"

"I stabbed her."

"What about the semen?" I knew that Stabler did not wear condoms during his first two sexual assaults.

He was livid. His face red, his eye twitching. I thought he was going to make me punish him, but he finally said, "We had sex."

"Consensual?"

"No."

"That's not sex then," I said. "You raped her, didn't you?"

"Yes," he said.

"Say it."

"I raped her."

"Then killed her."

"Then killed her."

"Say it."

"I raped her, and then I killed her."

I put the picture back in the folder. "See. That wasn't so bad. Man, if looks could kill, you'd be dropping nukes on me. Calm down, Stabby. We have five more girls in here." I took out the next photo. "This is Trisha Yarborough."

"I killed her," he said immediately. "She was one of my neighbors, too. I never played with her, though, so it was hard to get her to go with me. I told her I found a puppy, and she could have it. I took her to my grandmother's basement, and I killed her and I raped her."

"How did you—"

"I stabbed her," he said. "I tried to hide her body in the creek, but there was too much blood. I was filthy, and the basement was covered in blood. It was stupid. I got caught the same day."

"And that's when they found out you killed the first one... Lacy, right?"

"Yes."

I slid the photo back inside the envelope and took out the picture of Amy Winslet.

"You're a twisted fuck, but I got to give you credit for your honesty. Who is this?" I asked.

Stabler shook his head stubbornly. "I'm not doing it."

I frowned. "C'mon, killer. I thought we had a deal."

He was steaming. "Fuck you, man! You're twisted. You're the one who's fucked up. I'm not doing this shit anymore!" Apparently he wasn't as dehydrated as I thought. Sweat skated down his face in rivers.

This was going to be the second time he confessed to Amy's murder, and I knew it would be like pulling teeth. As I mentioned earlier, the first confession was recorded. But there was a glaring problem: The police tape starts with Stabler in the middle of a sentence, and there is no clear beginning. No one announces the date, time or introduces themselves. More importantly, no one reads Stabler his rights.

The detectives who interviewed him swore that they did read the Miranda. They said that, unbeknownst to them, their recording equipment was malfunctioning, and it only started working properly midway through their questioning.

They testified that they didn't know they missed the first part of his confession until they viewed the tapes later. But by then it was too late. Stabler changed his mind after the questioning, and he refused to sign his confession. His lawyer got the tapes thrown out fairly easily.

I knew getting him to own up to this murder a second time was going to be our first stumbling block, and I was prepared for a little resistance. I calmly put the photo away, stood with pliers in hand, and I closed the distance between us.

"What, what are you. Hey, hey *hold on*, man – *Wait!*"

I ignored him. I grabbed his right hand and steadied it as best I could while I clamped down on one of his fingernails with the pliers. He struggled a lot, and I think I got as much finger*tip* as I did nail, but that was okay.

I was under the impression that a whole fingernail would come off smoothly, but that's not the case. I had to let go of his wrist and use both hands on the pliers to get it off. His screams filled the room like sirens in a tunnel.

I sat back down in my chair.

"*You son of a bitch! You motherfucker! What the fuck is wrong with you? What the fuck, man? What the fuck?!*" Stabler craned his neck to try to get a look at his hand. The finger was squirting blood. Profusely. I knew there were no major veins in the finger tip, but the blood belied this knowledge.

"What'd you do?! What *did you do?!*" Stabler was livid, his eyes wild. Saliva spilled from his mouth, past his bruised lips, and dribbled down his chin. He struggled with all his might to free himself from the chair, but except for his head, he couldn't move any part of his body more than an inch.

The tape recorder fell from his chest. It slid down his side, and I had to get up and reach under his back to retrieve it. It was still running.

"I took your finger nail off," I said calmly. I wasn't calm, though. My own heart was racing as if I was in that chair. I hated this man more than anything I've ever despised, and I'd been planning this very moment for more than a year, but it was still pretty intense, as you can imagine.

PLAN C (AND MORE KWB SHORTS)

The blood and the screams put it all into perspective: I was really torturing this man. Me – a forty-year-old accountant from Iowa. I didn't think I'd have it in me to continue, but I had only to think about what he did to my little girl to find motivation. Her crime scene photos would always be somewhere in my mind.

"*What'd you do to me?*" Stabler screamed again.

"I pulled off your fingernail. The one on your pointer finger. I got mostly nail, but I got some skin off the tip, too." I held up the pliers to show him the disgusting plug of bloody flesh still gripped in its claws.

"*You're sick, man! You're fucking sick!*"

"You need to calm down, Stabby. It didn't have to go like that. *You* made it like that. Now..." I held up the picture again. "Who is this?"

"*Stop, man! Just stop. This is crazy. You're going to jail. You can't get a confession like this!*"

"Calm down, Ben, or I'm getting those spiders." He piped down right away. His chest rose and fell at unsafe intervals. "Now, who is this?" I asked again.

Stabler shook his head fiercely and yelled into the recorder, "*This is duress! This man, Mr. Barrett, has kidnapped me! Anything I say is under duress! This is not a proper confession. I am being held against my will. He has just attacked me with a pair of pliers! I'm bleeding...*"

I let him rant for awhile as I adjusted the vice grips. I tightened them until there was less than a quarter inch space between the teeth, about the height of two stacked nickels. I then leaned forward and clamped them down on his big toe until they locked.

"***Aaaaaaaah!***" He screamed like he was on fire. "*Take it off! Take it off!*"

I got up and walked closer to him. I stood on his right side.

"*Take it off, man! Take it off!*" He whipped his head back and forth like the girl in the *Exorcist*. He looked like he was being electrocuted.

"Listen, man–"

"*Take it off! Please! Take it off!*"

"No, you calm down and listen!"

"*Please! I'll do it! I'll do it!*"

"I know you're going to do it. But not like that."

"Take it off!"

"You can tell the police whatever you want when you get out of here," I said. "But you're not saying all of that on *my* tape. You're going to identify the girls and tell me what you did with them. *That's it.* You're messing up my confession. Now, do you want me to take those vice grips off?"

"Yes. *Please.* Take it off. *Take it off!"*

"Alright, Stabber, but you say only what I want you to. What happened to the girls. What you did with them. How you killed them. How you raped them. Where you put them. *That's it.* None of that extracurricular shit about me attacking you. I don't even want to hear my name in the tape, you understand?"

I had to dig the tape from beneath him again. I rewound it. Before I put it back on his chest, I gave him a stern warning: "If you mess up my recording again, I'm taking another nail and squishing another toe. Do you understand?"

"*Yes,*" he said. *"Please, just take it off."*

I did. To this date, I've never seen a toe as brutalized as that one was.

≈≈≈≈≈≈≈

I made him start all over with Lacy River's murder. In his state of shock, Stabler provided me more details than before. He talked about her for thirty minutes alone. I learned things that were not in any police or case report. I learned things I really didn't want to know, like his reasoning, motivation, fears and desires. His whole thought process was *skewed.* I knew he was crazy, but listening to him rationalize his actions made me nauseous. Lacy was nine years old. Trisha Yarborough, his second victim, was ten.

He took me through Amy Winslet's murder. Again he told me things that were not in any public records, like how he promised to call her father for her after the assault. He still remembered the phone number the girl gave him.

He told me that it *was* him who was seen leaving the mall with Tabitha Cage. He told her that her mommy was hurt and he was going to take her to the hospital. He knew her full name, her mother's name and their home address. He also knew what kind of car her mother drove as well as where she worked. Tabitha didn't get suspicious until they drove past the city limits, and she didn't confront the man whom she thought was her mother's friend until they were still driving when night fell.

Stabler told me where he took his last four victims, like Samantha Pierce, who was indeed in his vehicle – caught on camera by a traffic light. He had a small cabin on the outskirts of Des Moines. The cabin belonged to his grandmother and was willed to him when he was only three years old. The court papers had long since been lost or forgotten, and even Stabler's parents had never been there.

He visited the cabin shortly after being released from the mental hospital at the age of 21, and he promptly declared the place a piece of shit. Overgrown and unattended, he thought the shack would fall in on itself in another couple of years. Disenchanted, Stabler abandoned all hopes of living there. There were no neighbors for miles and no roads leading to it. You would literally have to hike half a mile to get to it.

Stabler never tried to sell the place, never had any utilities turned on there, and never kept any paperwork regarding it. The cabin was pretty much forgotten by the world until he met Amy Winslet ten years later and realized he did have use for it. This is the place where he confined and molested and murdered his last four victims, including my daughter, Lindsey Barrett.

When pressed, Stabler admitted that there was plenty of evidence in the cabin that would connect him to the girls, but he assured me I would never find the place. No search of his records would have any information about it. And if I *did* manage to locate it based on information received during this farce of a confession, it would become inadmissible in court.

Stabler was a smart man, but he didn't realize that I had no intentions of searching for the cabin or turning his confession over to the police. As a matter of fact, there wasn't even a tape in the recorder.

≈≈≈≈≈≈≈

When he was done, I stood on unstable legs. Tears streamed down my face, and my chest heaved uncontrollably. I knew it would be bad, but not that bad. I'd wanted to know what happened to my daughter ever since she didn't come home from band practice six years ago. But at the same time, I suppose I didn't *really* want to know.

What this man did to my daughter was perverse, disgusting and foul, and I listened to every word. As with the other murders, Stabler told me things about my daughter's case that were not in the public records. No one but the killer knew that not only had Lindsey been stabbed, but her nipples were sliced off. No one but the killer knew that with her last breaths Lindsey had called out to me. Not with "Daddy," or "Richard" (my first name), but she had whispered a name I hadn't heard since I dressed like a clown to surprise her on her 4th birthday.

Help me, Bozo.

I could barely walk, but I managed to make it out of the room. I leaned on every wall and didn't think I would make it outside before breaking down. The whole world spun around me. The hallways leaned this way and that way. My daughter's face was engrained on everything, but it wasn't her school pictures. The crime scene photos danced before my eyes, and I couldn't get her voice out of my head. I never even heard the words, but I could hear them then.

Help me, Bozo.

The factory was small. I burst through the lone metal door and sucked in a breath of air that wasn't foul and stale for the first time in four hours. I fell to my knees and cried right there. It was a loud, pained and slobbering cry that just kept coming. I cried not only for Lindsey, but for all of those girls who had the misfortune of growing up in the same city the Boogey Man lived in.

I don't know how long I was out there, but it must have been a long time, because when I could hear anything above my own wretched sorrow, Stabler was yelling; foolishly begging for his execution.

"Hey! You still there?"

Oh, I'm still here, I thought.

I didn't have a watch on, but the sun was still high in the sky. It looked to be no later than one pm. I got up and staggered to the dusty Buick Skylark I had parked in the shrubs nearby. All of the implements of torture I planned on using were already inside, but I decided that I was going to need the generator and lamps after all.

PLAN C (AND MORE KWB SHORTS)

With daylight-savings time in effect, the sun was going to set around 6:30. Five hours did not seem like enough time for all of the torment I wanted to put Stabler through. Five hours was not nearly enough.

≈≈≈≈≈≈≈

Wow.

If you just read this story, you most likely think I'm some kind of *monster*. I know how you feel. I just read the same story, and I'm wondering what kind of person I was back then myself. That's not to say that I wouldn't kill Stabler if I could go back in time, because I most certainly would. I'm just saying that, looking back on it all, my behavior may come off as shocking and appalling. And rightly so.

The whole experience was similar to a woman who lifts a car to free her trapped child. I don't know where I found the strength and wherewithal to do what I did, but I'm sure I could do it again if need be.

I wrote my accounts of that horrific day twenty-five years ago. I didn't write it for any fortune or fame. On the contrary, I wrote it with hopes that it would never be read. It *is* evidence, after all. As good as a signed confession, it links me directly to the death of Benjamin Frederick Stabler.

In truth, I wrote these accounts for my family and friends. If I were ever prosecuted for the crime, which at the time seemed like a good possibility, they could read it and know why I did what I did. Maybe it would give them some insight into my state of mind, and they could find it in their hearts to forgive me.

I put the letter in a safe deposit box at the post office and instructed my attorney to present it to my family upon such a time as my untimely demise or lengthy incarceration. He was curious about the incarceration clause, but he didn't press for details.

I watch TV as much as the next guy, and I know it's pretty much impossible to get away with murder these days, especially one as messy as the one I committed. I was sure the detectives would be knocking at my door any moment. When I got back to Iowa, I jumped every time the doorbell rang for the first three months. Seriously. I didn't feel comfortable about any of it for at least ten years.

There's a myriad of emotions you go through with something like this. At first I was somewhat proud of what I did and nonplused about going to jail. I knew I did wrong, and I would take responsibility for my actions.

But as time went by and I wasn't even questioned by the police, I started to think, *Hey, I might actually get away with this.* That's when it started to get hard for me. The longer I remained free, the more I wanted to remain free. After a while, I was totally against the idea of going to prison. I thought I'd experienced stress before, but I had no idea. The emotional roller coaster I put myself on started to feel like I was already on death row. The worst point came when they found the Murder Man's body.

≈ ≈ ≈ ≈ ≈ ≈

I tortured Stabler for quite a while that fateful day, well into the night and a little bit more the following morning. He begged for mercy. He pleaded for me to put him out of his misery more times than I can count. I asked him if he'd shown any of his six victims any mercy. I talked about the girls the whole time. I reminded him that he'd cut off my daughter's nipples as I cut off his. He sodomized all of his victims but thought I was going too far when I used my lead pipe to do the same to him.

I won't go into any further details about this. I'm an old man, and it's embarrassing. Unless you're taking notes for a gruesome murder you plan to commit one day, it really serves no purpose to divulge. I'll just say that before his death, Stabler endured pain and suffering in every way imaginable. He experienced things that were unimaginable, too.

When I was done, the place was a mess. My original plan was to take his body to an alternate location for disposal. But since it was going to be clear to anyone who saw the room that *someone* had been murdered there, I decided not to move him. The room was totally concrete, and this worked to my advantage. I waited until nightfall to set the fire. It was too dark to see the smoke, and if anyone smelled it, they didn't call it in. I managed to keep the fire localized in that one room, and thankfully I didn't burn down the whole building or any surrounding greenery.

Later, I drove all the way back to Iowa in the stolen Buick. And let me tell you, that was a *long* drive. Every time I stopped for gas, I knew that I was digging a hole for myself, and it was getting deeper and deeper. I paid at the pump each time with one of the untraceable Visa cards. I was thinking, *The less people who saw me, the better*, but I knew there were cameras at most of those gas stations.

If Stabler's body was found immediately, and I became a suspect, the detectives would be able to track my movements all the way to Texas and back. What I was banking on was them not being able to find his body for a long, long time. Once again fate was on my side.

Benjamin Stabler was reported missing a week after his disappearance, and this was big news. The immediate speculation was that he had gone to some far away place where no one knew him; a place where he might rape and murder another innocent girl, perhaps. Of course the media chose to sensationalize the story with grave warnings: *Mr. Murder's on the loose! Lock your doors*! and what not.

The average missing person would get a report filed and maybe a poster at Walmart, but Stabler got what looked like the whole National Guard on his case, which is why they found the blood in his driveway and began to suspect foul play. Like I said, I dropped him once when I was loading him into the trunk. I didn't think there was any blood at the scene, but it was dark. I began to wonder what else I missed.

They found the burnt Buick in Altoona a few weeks later. That didn't make the local news, but I found the story tucked in the back of their local paper. To this day, I don't believe the police have ever made a connection between that car and the missing serial killer.

For the most part, the popular consensus was that someone had killed Stabler. Beating trial when most of the world was convinced he was a killer, made Stabler more notorious than O.J. Simpson. Stabler didn't have the popularity factor O.J. had, so killing him would have been a much simpler task. Being the father of one of his murder victims, a father who had been on *Oprah* ranting about how unfair it had all been, made me a suspect, of course. But if the police ever put me on a list, they never went public with it.

The media, on the other hand, thought my possible involvement was all too juicy. They started calling and following me around again, like they did when Stabler first beat the trial. I even got an offer for a book deal. If I agreed, they would give me a quarter million dollars. I didn't even have to write it; they just wanted me to say I wrote it. They wanted to title the book, *"If I Killed Stabler, This is How I Did It."* Of course I graciously declined that offer and kept denying any involvement.

I allayed most of the suspicion by simply giving the cameras what they wanted. I told them that if Stabler *was* dead, then it was a good thing, because in my opinion, he was the murderer of my little girl. I told them, *"I hope he's rotting in hell."* When the headlines read, *"Grieving Father Hopes Stabler is Dead,"* this is what was expected of me, and I think it helped to remove the spotlight a little. There were five other grieving fathers who felt the same way I did.

They didn't find Stabler's body for another ten years. I was fifty years old by then but not too old to go to prison. So, as you might assume, I followed these developments closely. Apparently a young skateboarding fanatic named Stephen McBain was tired of being harassed by security guards and mall cops for practicing his tricks on public property.

He decided to check out a piece of land that had been willed to him over several generations in hopes of leveling whatever structure was there so he could build his own skate park. Stephen took a few friends with him to check the place out, and they were quick to call 911 and report, *"Dude, we found, like, this mummy guy."*

Once again I had a problem. Stabler's body was burnt crispy, but without any direct sunlight, it had not decayed as much as I would have liked. They were able to extract DNA from the corpse, and after finding no matches from the many missing person cases in Texas, they entered the profile into a national database and got a hit. Once again there was a media firestorm, and once again reporters wanted to get everyone's opinion about finally getting confirmation on Stabler's death.

Even with the scant evidence available, it was clear that he had been tortured, so I knew it was only a matter of time before my phone started ringing again. When it did, I reiterated my previous statements: I told them I was glad he was dead, and if someone tortured him, then that was what he deserved. I thought the police would call for sure this time, but they never did. They never found anyone else's DNA in the factory, only Benjamin Stabler's.

≈≈≈≈≈≈≈

So here we are. Another six years have passed, and nothing's changed. I'm sixty-five years old now, and I no longer live in fear of my impending doom. The police have long-since admitted that they are pretty stumped with the case, and all requests for public assistance have yielded no fruit. They have no suspects and have exhausted all leads. I'm sure they have speculations about what happened in that pickle factory twenty-five years ago, and some of their theories may include me. But anything they have must be circumstantial. Apparently they can't drag me into an interrogation room simply because I had a motive. The whole world had a motive.

As for me, I've come to terms with what I did and have long since asked God for forgiveness. I don't know if I can truly be forgiven if I don't have remorse, but that is a technicality I will have to work out with the man upstairs when we meet face to face.

Lindsey was my youngest daughter. My other two have since married and given me the most beautiful grandchildren in the world. My first wife left me shortly after Lindsey's body was found. Our relationship had been rocky for years. I suppose we didn't have enough love left to comfort each other when we needed it the most.

I've remarried and will celebrate my 13th anniversary this fall. My wife has never asked me if I had anything to do with Stabler's disappearance or death, and I have never volunteered the tale, either.

This manuscript is going back in my safe deposit box, I suppose. I may request that it is destroyed upon my death, but a part of me wants to leave it for the world. It's not that I want any kind of posthumous attention. I just think I should offer some finality to the story of Benjamin Stabler.

I can't tell you how big this thing has gotten. All of those baffled detectives would sure like some closure. And all of the books and movies have been pointing fingers at the wrong people for a long time. There are more theories about the identity of Stabler's killer than there are about who Jack the Ripper was. A few crazies have even confessed to killing Stabler, but none of them were credible enough to get locked up, thank God.

In case you're wondering, I did feel bad about stealing that Buick. I sent the family a blank money-order for $5,000, even though, according to the Official Kelley Blue Book, the vehicle was worth no more than fifteen-hundred at the time I stole it.

Like I told you, I'm not a monster.

SOILED DOVE

Betty Cotton wore a very short dress with no panties. She sat on the bed in room 14B and sucked hard on a glass pipe, taking what one in the know would refer to as a *monster hit*. One in the know would also tell you that crack cocaine is a legitimately horrible drug, regardless of the dosage, but monster hits upped the ante even more. Monster hits came with *Felix the Cat* warnings; you'll sweat too much, your chest will ache, your heart will go pitty-pat. Betty was aware that this could be her last drag on the pipe, but every domicile she burglarized and every trick serviced or robbed might be her last. *That* stuff was risky business. Crack was the reward. Crack was the recliner with the television remote at the end of a hard day's work.

Betty lay back on the bed, careful not to burn herself or the sheets with her glass pipe. The immediate rush of cocaine causes users to do odd things. All crack smokers have some type of *skitz*. Most involve an overwhelming and irrational fear that someone is out to get you. Users will creep around their own home, checking the peepholes and peeping through the curtains for hours.

Betty's skitz was not so dramatic. She liked to lie across the bed and stare at the ceiling. Most ceilings had textures, and they could be as brilliant as a Rembrandt painting to the right eyes. The ceiling in room 14B was weird. It was either sloppy workmanship or some variation of the *slap brush* or *panda paw* technique. Betty dated a handyman once and learned more than she wanted to know on the subject of dry-walling. Some people see you staring at a ceiling and think you want to know everything about it. Others see you lying on your back and think, *Surely she must want a penis inside of her. Surely.*

This is why Betty preferred to get high alone.

Selling sex was simple, merely a means to an end, but how other whores managed to enjoy their high with a room full of people was amazing. Betty wouldn't even get high with a John in the room with her. They were too nosey. Too grabby. Getting high with other smokers was even worse. Most crackheads don't know how to sit their asses down and be quiet. They get on their hands and knees and search for tiny crumbs of crack on the floor. They beg. A bona fide dopefiend will ask, *"Did you hear that?"* so many times, you'll start hearing it yourself.

Betty liked to get a motel room by herself and enjoy a simulation of happiness as the drug increased her heart rate to clinically unsafe levels, and her brain solidified its love affair with cocaine. Betty was only twenty-seven, but she already deemed herself a professional when it came to smoking crack. Everything had to be just so. She took great lengths to ensure distractions would be minimized, which is why she was surprised to hear someone knocking at her motel room's only door.

Betty's legs were dangling over the side of the bed. She swirled her big toe on the carpet. Most people wouldn't dare walk barefoot in a seedy motel room, but for the most part, Betty lived in motels. If she couldn't walk barefoot at home, then life would truly suck. Her toenails were painted but beginning to chip. The fuchsia polish was flattering to her skin tone; a smooth mix of honey and caramel. She wore a thin, gold ankle bracelet that had a small panda at the clasp.

Her first inclination was to ignore the visitor. It was only a little after midnight, but Betty already enjoyed a profitable day. She had enough dope to get her through the night and enough money to buy more when she woke up. Even if the visitor benefited her, it was probably not worth the trouble. Except, maybe it was. Because when you're a dopefiend, opportunity is your best friend.

Opportunity knocked again.

There was really no question as to whether she would answer the door or not. If one of her friends simply wanted to get out of the environment, they were welcome, but there was a price for that. Betty sat up and wrapped her glass pipe in a napkin. The pipe was beautiful to her. It was sacred. She'd been using it for three days, and it was caked with cocaine residue. She put it in her purse and rose with the stately air of a princess. The *Crack Wheel of Fortune* was spinning, and Betty was rooting for *Big Money! Big Money!*

She wore a tan sundress. It had orange patterns that reminded her of fall. Betty had a good number of sundresses. Most of the hookers who stalked the lonely streets of Overbrook Meadows preferred tighter and more scant outfits, but Betty ensured her dresses were always slutty by keeping the length *way* too short. Always too short. Standing, the hem barely inched past the split between her legs. Sitting, the dress hiked halfway up her ass. On the streets, she could cause traffic accidents.

Betty stood 5'1" and wore her hair short like Halle Berry's in *Swordfish*. She was thin but not sickly with small breasts and smooth legs. Most of her customers would go on and on about her physique, but Betty always thought her eyes were her best feature. She attempted modeling as a teenager, but she was too short to make it very far. When she got to the door, Betty had to stand on her tip-toes to look out of the peephole. No one was there.

"Who is it?" she yelled. She waited a beat. There was no answer. Betty was about to open the door when a response came.

"Uh, h-hello?" It was a male's voice, not deep, but mature. A tall figure came into view from the left. The darkness prevented a detailed description, but Betty could see that her visitor was fair-skinned, over six feet, and he wore a beard. He gazed downwards, as if he was unaware of the peephole.

"What you want?" Betty asked. He didn't look like anyone she knew. She thought she had made the acquaintance of every dopefiend and drug dealer in the neighborhood.

"Hey, uh," the man kept his head down, "I'm looking for this lady," he said. Most of the men who propositioned her did so with similar hesitance, so this didn't qualify as odd behavior in Betty's world.

"What lady?" she asked.

The man stalled again. He looked around a bit, still more sheepish than strange.

"I don't know her name," he admitted. "I saw her earlier, around here. She's like, light-skinned. Got on a, a brown dress."

The stranger had the right room, but he still hadn't answered either of Betty's questions. "Who are you?" she asked with her crabbiest voice. "And what you want?"

"It's you?" her visitor asked, looking up for the first time. Betty was surprised to see that he was mildly handsome. He would never be confused with Will Smith, but given the location and the late hour, she was pleased that he was not the boogeyman. Betty had met the most horrendous people in this city after midnight.

"Who are you?" she asked again.

"I'm, uh," he looked down again, "Tommy."

"Mmm hmmm," she breathed. "Well, what you want, *Tommy*?"

He shifted his weight from one foot to the other. "I wanna see you," he said after a short pause.

"What the hell you want?" Betty asked again.

"I just, man, can't you open the door? I feel weird talking out here like this. What if the police come by? I got some money."

Ca-ching! Betty released the deadbolt and opened the door. There was a small step at the threshold. Tommy already stood a foot taller than her without making use of it. He looked Betty up and down and smiled brightly.

The stranger had a large gap between his bunny rabbit teeth. His hair was short and mostly black, but there was a good deal of gray sprinkled throughout. His beard was trimmed neatly. He had a big, wide nose with nostrils large enough to stick a thumb in without much stretching. His thick brows shaded large eyes that appeared even larger as he took in Betty's physique. She guessed he was 50, but it was a strong, healthy 50, like Wesley Snipes.

Tommy wore a long-sleeved shirt with a button-down collar. The shirt wasn't tucked in, but wrinkle lines around the bottom indicated it had been at some point earlier in the day. He stuck a meaty hand into his front pocket and produced three twenty-dollar bills. He held them out to the hooker and then brought his hand back a little when she didn't snatch it.

"I got some more, if this ain't enough."

Betty looked at the money. "What you wanna do with that?" she asked him.

Tommy blushed. Betty grinned as he stammered.

"I, uh..." He looked around. "Oh, shit. Don't tell me this the wrong room. I thought you was..."

"C'mon," Betty said, backing up to allow him entrance.

Tommy stepped into the room quickly, closing the door behind himself. "You want me to do the bolt?" he asked.

"Yeah," Betty said. She backed up to the bed and sat down with her legs crossed. Tommy stood five feet away. He turned from the door and was immediately captivated by her thighs. Betty thought he had pretty eyes.

"What's your name?" he asked her.

"Ebony," she said. "Where you know me from?"

"I saw you earlier," Tommy said. "I saw you, I think, maybe around five. I was gon' stop then, but I was with somebody. But when I saw you..." He shook his head. "I wanted to stop. You look, you're a very good looking woman, Ebony."

She smiled. She uncrossed her legs and then crossed them again, a la *Basic Instinct*, but Tommy got a better look at her goodies than Sharon Stone's fans had. The look on his face was priceless. Betty was reminded of a goal she had. She wanted to create a portfolio with pictures of different men as they made that look, that, *Ooh, that kitty look good*, look. No matter what kind of man it is, that look is always the same. It excited Betty to the point that she was already becoming moist for him.

"So, what you talking 'bout spending?" she asked.

Overbrook Meadows was a large but not blatantly wealthy city, and the Economy Inn was located in the worst ghetto. Hookers in Las Vegas might get three to five hundred a trick, but the crackheads had sullied the game in this city. Betty was constantly picked up by men who thought twenty dollars was a good trade for a blow-job *and* sex. Mr. Tommy had already offered sixty, but Betty hoped to squeeze him for twice that amount.

The stranger produced two more twenties. "I got a hundred," he said. "If that's not enough..." He trailed off and reached towards his back pocket.

Betty was eager to relieve him of the hundred dollars, but she would never agree to the first offer.

"What you wanna do?" she asked. "If you just want some head, then you got enough." Betty sweetened the deal. "You want me to suck your dick, baby?" Dirty talk was the best and the most overlooked weapon of the prostitute. "You want me to get that nut outta you?"

Tommy smiled. Betty thought she could slide a nickel between the gap in his teeth.

"I like you," he said. "I *knew* I was gon' like you! I knew it when I drove by earlier. I knew you was the one."

"C'mon, daddy," Betty said, leaning back on the bed. Propped up by her elbows, she went for the jackpot. In a calculated move, her legs came apart slightly and she hunched her hips forward, making the skirt ride back towards her waist. Tommy stared at her pubic hairs and was nearly belligerent in his pursuit. He surged forward.

Betty snapped her legs closed and halted the trick's forward progress with a stiff arm to his chest. "Naw, baby," she cooed. "You said you had that hundred for head. You want it all, you gotta pay more."

She might have been pushing too far, but Betty felt she had him on a string. He'd seen it, smelled it and was merely inches from touching it. Tommy wanted it. He wanted it bad, and he would have it, regardless of the cost.

When he fell on top of her, Betty's first thought was that he was having some sort of heart attack or seizure. His face went slack, his body limp, and he simply fell. It was dead weight. There seemed to be no tense muscles in his body. Betty had seen people die before, and she knew that sometimes there is no warning when it's time to go be with Jesus.

Did this fool have a heart attack? Her tease wasn't that severe, but who knew how long it had been since the old fart saw a naked woman?

Betty sighed, looking around anxiously. She wondered if she should report the incident to the manager's office or simply leave the motel. They had her I.D. information. If she left, would the police would come looking for her immediately, or would they do an autopsy first? She wondered how hard it was going to be to dig herself from beneath her unlucky date. She wondered why his dead fingers were making their way towards her throat. And then she understood everything.

Tommy lifted his head from her bosom, and Betty understood something else. Those eyes, they were not as pretty as she thought. Once you got good and close to them, those eyes were downright ugly. His beard brushed her nose. It smelled of lemon. A vague scent of stale coffee rolled past his lips. He didn't speak at all.

Betty struggled as much as she could, but her right arm was pinned between her attacker's chest and her own stomach. She used her left hand to beat at his face and shoulder, but she couldn't get the necessary leverage to make the punches hurt. She wanted to gouge out his eyes, but it was getting harder and harder to make her hand do what she wanted it to. The trick's initial fall had forced most of the breath from Betty's lungs, and no oxygen was incoming. His thumbs found a home at the front of her throat, and the pressure increased.

Betty was surprised to realize that she hadn't even screamed. She tried it now, but much like her air supply, that window of opportunity had closed. She felt as if her windpipe was bended like a plastic straw. Her mouth fell open, and tears squirted from her eyes.

Betty wondered what the fuck was going on here. What kind of rapist brought money, and what part of rape did this guy not understand? There was supposed to be blows to the head, threats with a weapon and what not. But this guy was killing her. Did he not know that she was going to die?

Can't get no pussy that way, 'less you like it dead.

Betty didn't know why, but that was funny to her. She couldn't help but smile. She smiled and thought of cotton candy as her eyes rolled to the back of her head and the room went completely black.

Cotton candy? Betty frowned. She always thought crack would be the last thing on her mind.

≈≈≈≈≈≈≈

Thomas Hudgens almost shit his pants when she opened the door. It was *her*, and she had on that same dress. That dress had to be illegal. The whore couldn't go outside on a windy day without exposing her disgusting cooch. That dress shouldn't even be allowed inside, but she wore it outside. In *public*. Little kids saw her in that dress. Grandmothers saw her. Whores were out of control these days.

Tommy hated her.

He hated all of her.

He hated the way she walked with her head up high, as if selling ass was all of a sudden a noble profession. He hated her short hair. He hated her pretty face. He hated her whore legs. Tommy hated all of the whores in Overbrook Meadows, but he hated this one the most. His rage was crippling.

Standing on her stoop, he dared not look at the peephole, lest she see his eyes. He could not conceal his wrath, so he played it off as nervousness. He thought she'd see through this (whores have a sixth sense for danger nowadays), but she let him in anyway. She smiled at him and spread her nasty legs open for him.

Tommy had to fight to keep his supper down. Who would want that disgusting hole? It stank. He didn't have to get close to it to know that it stank. They all stank. AIDS filled pus holes. Tommy wished he could twist a knife in that hole, but the thought of her fluids touching him was revolting.

He wanted to prolong her death. He wanted it to be a masterpiece, like the one in Midland. He wanted her to answer a few pointed questions like *Do you know you're a whore? You're a whore, aren't you? Do you know what happens to whores?* He wanted to make her suffer, to pull her nipples off with his bare hands. But God! Her arrogance. Who the hell did she think she was?

He lunged for her. Startled by the ease of her immobilization, he lay on top of her for a few awkward moments. The whole room reeked, but she stank the worse. She was abhorrent to him. His stomach rolled. Her whole body smelled like sex. Her hair smelled like sex. Sweat dripped from her pores, and even it stank like sex.

The hooker's struggle was minimal, but it was enough to knock over her purse and send a couple of items spilling from it. There was Blistex, a few coins and mascara. But it was her keychain that caught Tommy's eye. It tumbled out and came to a rest near her right shoulder. The sight of it made Tommy's fingers grow cold and stiff around the whore's jugular. Still squeezing, he leaned closer to the keychain, but the picture attached to it did not change. It was Lela. There was absolutely no doubt about it. It was her.

Tommy's mouth was suddenly very dry. His grip loosened. The whore didn't move, and neither did he. The only sounds were his soft breaths and jagged heartbeats. He removed his hands. Fresh wounds sprouted on the prostitute's neck and quickly reddened. She wasn't breathing. Still straddling her, Tommy reached with trembling fingers and plucked her keychain from the bed. There was a small picture holder connected to the main ring. Inside the holder was the picture of Lela.

The photo was a little smaller than the one he received through the mail, but it was from the same studio session. In prison, there was little for Tommy to do but read his letters repeatedly and stare at his pictures. Those pictures were what kept him connected to the outside world. This particular picture was tattooed on his soul. It was the same silly springtime background. Lela wore the same Winnie the Pooh jumpsuit. She was smiling the greatest smile a granddaughter could smile. Tommy had always seen a little of himself in that smile.

He rose to his feet.

The keys fell to the floor with a muffled *clink*. Tommy swayed on shaky legs. Something heavy fell from his chest and settled low in his belly. He stared at the whore in confusion. Why did she have Lela's picture? It was not possible that this – this *thing* had created his granddaughter. Tommy refused to believe that. But how could he know for sure?

He received Lela's picture in the mail a little over a year ago. His sister sent it to him. She was the only person who maintained regular visits while Tommy did his time at Ft. Leavenworth penitentiary. Tommy's relationship with his son was rocky, but other family members kept him abreast of what was going on in the free world. While in prison, Tommy received precious little information about the woman who bore his grandchild, but no one told him she was whore.

Tommy had only seen the one photo of his granddaughter, and Lela was the most beautiful thing he'd every laid eyes on. He looked down and could not deny that the prostitute was attractive as well.

Tommy's stomach churned. His heart rattled in the back of his throat. He backed away from the bed. The whore's dress was hiked up to her belly. He resisted an urge to cover her shame. Tommy didn't raise his son, but he thought the boy had better sense. Had he procreated with this woman while she was in this lifestyle? Tommy doubted this prostitute was a productive member of society two years ago. Was his son on drugs as well? Where was his granddaughter now, while her mother whored her life away in these seedy motels? Why didn't anyone tell him that his son's baby-mama was a crack whore?

The prostitute emitted a strained whistling noise. Watching her chest rise and fall, Tommy saw that she was indeed alive. Her belly swelled big as she took in a much needed breath of air. Tommy had to fight a passionate urge to mount her and complete his work. She would have been his fifth masterpiece. She was the most beautiful. Her death would have been exquisite, but he couldn't do it – not to his granddaughter's mother. That would be appalling, even for him.

Outside, it was not yet one am. Walking away from room 14B, Tommy was almost immediately engulfed in darkness. No one had seen him come, and likewise no eyes spied him as he departed. There were no working cameras at the Economy Inn, as was the case with a good number of these pay by the hour motels. Tommy had no fear of repercussions. And he still had five twenty dollar bills. The night was young. There was time to find another. Still plenty of time.

≈≈≈≈≈≈≈

Betty Cotton regained consciousness at 3:22 am. She did not jerk awake with a start. Instead she swam to the world of the living. Swimming from such depths can be scary, but it was mostly comforting. She broke the surface a few times but was obliged to sink back into the abyss. The chasm of slumber was dark, but warm. Undefined, yet comforting.

When she finally did open her eyes, Betty found that the ceiling was still beautiful. It was as if someone had used many tiny brushes to – she sat up quickly and gripped at the fingers on her neck. They were gone, but memories of the attack flooded her mind, pounding like tidal waves. She remembered his touch, his smell. His eyes.

The scream she had been trying to summon during the attack finally escaped her lips. Betty jumped to her feet and staggered to the bathroom. The world was not stable. She had to lean heavily on the wall and then on the bathroom sink to avoid falling.

85

That motherfucker.

The mirror revealed the full extent of her trauma. Betty's eyes were dark and sunken in their sockets. Her lips were white. Her neck was bruised. A trail of blood snaked from her nostril to her right ear where it had puddled and dried while she was unconscious. She was ashen and haggard.

She turned on the water and jumped at the sound. It suddenly occurred to her that the attacker might still be nearby. He had not raped her, but what plans did he have? Betty didn't think anyone would simply strangle her – for no good reason. Was he on his way back? Was he still there?

That last thought was the springboard that got her moving. Betty turned off the water and listened for a few seconds. She couldn't hear anything over the frantic pounding of her own heart. Better judgment told her to leave *NOW*, but she couldn't go without her pipe. And if her attacker didn't rob her, then she still had three-hundred dollars.

Back in the main room, Betty emptied her purse onto the bed and quickly scavenged through its contents. Her money was still there, wrapped in the purple scrunchie she put around it. Her pipe was intact also. She didn't think she'd ever want to get high again, but simply holding it made her salivate.

Betty found one shoe, but she discarded it without dropping to her knees to look for the other one. The heels on those pumps were too high, and if she had to run, they would do her no good.

Thinking of nothing more she needed, Betty opened the door to room 14B slowly. There was no one standing there or hiding among the shadows. There was no sound, say a few horny crickets under the building. If her attacker was still out there, she might encounter him again. But he wouldn't have the luxury of surprise anymore. Betty would fight him for her life, *literally*, and if he did manage to kill her, he would wear the marks from the experience for years.

There was no need to dally, so she didn't. Betty hit the parking lot jogging. Two blocks later, she was sprinting on the cold, dark streets.

As she ran, Betty wondered if she should have left that purse on the bed. It was a nice purse, but it wasn't hers, per se. She stole it from a Laundromat earlier that day. Betty usually didn't steal from single mothers, but it was such an easy grab. She couldn't resist. Later, when she got to the room and went through the purse, Betty found the keychain with the baby's picture on it. The picture of the unknown child made her feel guilty again, but crackheads do things that make them feel bad everyday. Betty said a little prayer for the baby on the keychain, and she prayed for the woman she stole the purse from, too. But that was all she could do for them at that point.

In any event, there was no way she was going back for the pilfered purse. *The hell with it.* She knew it might end up in the hands of the police, and they would realize it was stolen, but surely the detectives had more important things to worry about, like catching a goddamned pervert killer!

Damn, what's wrong with people today, Betty wondered as she put more distance between herself and the motel. *A bitch can't never catch a break!*

PLAN C

I hung up the phone knowing my mom had done exactly what she said she had, which meant I had about fifteen minutes before they would be knocking at my door. Flustered, I rushed to the bedroom and kicked Ryan's mattress. He rolled over lazily and brought a hand up to shade his face. It was well after noon but still early for us. Two or three was a more respectable time to get out of bed.

"Whah?" he said.

"Dude, you are not going to believe what my mom did!"

"Whah?" he said again.

"She sent the cops over here, man!"

"What?" Ryan sat up with a start.

"Yeah," I confirmed. "She said the constable went over there looking for me, and she told him I was over here."

"Damn, dude. That's fucked up. You *serious*?"

"Yeah," I said, heading towards the closet.

Sitting on the side of his bed, Ryan looked forlorn. These were traffic citations I was wanted for. I only had to do about seven or eight days, tops. But Ryan looked depressed, as if I had a felony. He wore one sock, a pair of green boxers and a dirty wife-beater. Ryan's hair was dirty blonde. Not dirty-blonde, it was blonde and dirty. A day at the salon would do him some good, but who was I to suggest it? I was pretty disheveled myself.

We broke down two air conditioners yesterday, scavenging for copper. And though I bathed last night, my hands were still smudged with dark patches. Mom had awakened me with her call, and I wore only boxers and a white tee myself. But at least *my* shirt was clean. I sniffed it and realized that it wasn't.

"Hey, I thought you told her you were gonna go down there and see the judge or something," Ryan called.

"That was two months ago!" I reminded him.

"Oh, yeah. But she called the cops on you? Dude. That's your *mom!*"

I emerged from the closet, stepping into a pair of Dickey work pants. I lost my balance and fell against Ryan's dresser. He laughed.

"She got tired of all those letters going to her house," I told him. "She said it's better to go now than wait and get caught when I'm on my way somewhere important." My last *important* appointment was a dental visit three years ago. Ryan chuckled.

"Man, you think this is funny?"

"Naw. I'm just saying... What are you gonna do? You gonna *run?*" Ryan was five-foot-eight and weighed 156 pounds. He was about as far from a hardened criminal as you could get, but he was serious about me running. Ryan's last arrest started as a simple traffic stop for an expired registration sticker. Thirty miles and three counties later, he had beefed up a pretty good evading arrest charge.

"No, I'm not gonna run, *stupid.*"

Ryan asked, "Why not?"

"'Cause I won't get away. Nobody gets away when they run."

Ryan had to nod at this. *World's Wildest Police Chases* was our favorite show, especially when we were high.

"Anyway," I said, "if I do get away, I'll still have warrants. But if I let them take me to jail, I'll be free when I get out. I can get a job and everything." This was my *cup half full* spiel. Pulling off my dirty tee, I scooted back into the closet.

"So what are you gonna do?" Ryan asked. He was out of bed, heading for his bong.

"I'm going to jail," I called back. "Have you seen my sweater?"

"It's like, a hundred degrees outside," Ryan pointed out.

"Man, have you ever been to Tucker?" I asked, knowing that he had.

"It's *freezing* in there!" Ryan recalled. "Dude, you're going *there?* Just thinking about that place makes me cold." He shivered. "I hate that jail."

PLAN C (AND MORE KWB SHORTS)

Tucker County Jail is a holding facility for the many, *many* inmates arrested in our city, Overbrook Meadows, Texas. Our county jail is so overcrowded, to continue making arrests we have to pay another city to hold our prisoners. Almost everyone arrested in Overbrook Meadows could find themselves at the Tucker facility. The only way to avoid the place was to bond out immediately; otherwise you stayed there until your court date came about or until you served your time.

The Tucker jail is a rare place where sex offenders, murderers, and jaywalkers can find themselves sharing bunks and burgers. Anything could happen to you in Tucker, but you were *guaranteed* to be exposed to two things: Violence and near-freezing conditions. Rumor had it they kept it chilly enough to kill germs.

I emerged from the closet topless and saw that Ryan was preparing his bong.

"Fool, what are you doing?" I asked him.

"If you're going to jail, you're gonna need this," he explained.

That made sense, but first things first. "I have to get dressed," I calmly explained to him. "If I'm not dressed when they get here, you know they're not going to let me put anything on. Aren't you gonna help me?"

Ryan reluctantly put down his baggie of marijuana. "Okay. What do you want me to do?"

"I need a sweater," I said irritably. "Or a sweatshirt. And a couple of tee-shirts. Some new socks, too. And I wanna take your boots."

"You can't take the boots 'cause they're steel-toed. They'll make you wear plastic slippers if you take those. And you know we don't have any clean socks. Your Christmas sweater is in Ben's bed, I think."

"Ben's been eating my sweater?" I exclaimed.

"No, he's just sleeping on it. Look, you get the sweater, and I'll find you a couple of shirts. You want to wear my New Balances?"

"No," I said and headed out of the room. "I need something that won't fall off my feet without the shoelaces. I'll wear my high-tops."

Ben is the biggest Great Dane you'd ever want to meet. He looked like Marmaduke's big brother. I removed my sweater from under his torso, and he responded with a lazy fart.

Let me stop for a second to tell you who I am... My name is Wes, I'm twenty-one years old, and I live with my friend Ryan. He's twenty-two. I'm tall, bushy-haired, blue-eyed and surprisingly skinny. It's weird 'cause I gorge myself on a regular basis. Twinkies are close to the top of my food pyramid, and nachos count as a dairy product. I'm not a criminal, but I often find myself driving cars with bad tags. Well, I guess technically that does make me a criminal. *An unlucky one.* When I'm behind the wheel, cops will find me as surely as a dog will find his bone – which is why I'm going to jail.

Three minutes later I was fully dressed, and I didn't need Ryan to tell me I looked like a damned fool. I wore the black Dickey workpants with my blue and white Nike sneakers. I sported two tee shirts, one white and one green (both dirty), with my Christmas sweater pulled over them. The sweater was mostly red, and it had one of the seven dwarves on the front, Grumpy I think. He had his arms folded and his back turned on a beautifully decorated Christmas tree. Grumpy's nose pointed skywards, and the caption read, *"Bah! Humbug!"*

I grabbed a green jacket I planned to take, too. It was odd, but I actually felt good about going to jail that day. I'd been arrested twice, and each time I had to ball into a fetal position to escape the frost of those concrete floors. I knew my suffering would be lessened this time, and I knew my mom was right: It was better to just get it over with. I was never going to have enough money to pay for my tickets, so why not sit them out?

"You're gonna get your ass kicked," Ryan noted.

"Hurry and let me hit that," I told him.

≈ ≈ ≈ ≈ ≈ ≈

By the time the constable knocked on the door, I was plenty high and plenty warm. I put the jacket on before I undid the deadbolt, lest the policeman order me to leave it behind. The officer was short and stocky, and he wore a handlebar moustache. At 6'3", I towered over him head and shoulders. I smiled down at him.

"You Wesley Harris?" he asked, looking me over.

"My friends call me 'Wes'," I said.

"Let me see your I.D."

I produced my driver's license.

"Turn around, and put your hands behind your back," he ordered. "And take that *goddamned coat* off!"

≈≈≈≈≈≈

I was in the back of a patrol car headed downtown for the third time in two years, but I didn't consider myself a "bad kid." I can say that without pause because I've met some really bad kids in my lifetime, and I know I'm not one of them. I had a friend named Sammy who liked to sniff paint in the seventh grade. He was shooting heroin by high school. I once dated a girl who killed two people in a drunk-driving accident.

I merely found a fondness for *Mary Jane* during my junior year of high school, and I skipped too many classes to graduate on time. I did get my GED though, and since that diploma is *good enough*, I was still poised to take the world by storm. My roommate Ryan, on the other hand, is a bad kid by any standards.

Ryan's the kind of guy you want to grab hold of and shake the hell out of sometimes. His parents own the third largest pickle manufacturing company in the state, but he doesn't have a dime of his own money in the bank. Why? Because midway through his freshman year of high school, Ryan decided he wanted to take the rebellious, drug-addict route.

After six failed trips to rehab and more outings to the juvenile detention center than his parents wanted to remember, Ryan dropped-out of school and accepted his role as the proverbial black sheep. Ryan's younger sister and older brother both cruised the city in Benz's and Bentleys, but because of Ryan's insolence, there was no new car for him every year. We tooled around in a late model Chevy truck that had a severe oil leak.

One good thing about having Ryan as a friend was his always-faithful grandma. She wouldn't give Ryan money directly, but we lived in a three-bedroom home and never saw a house note or grocery bill. This enabling is why neither of us had punched a time-clock in six months. Our only driving need was daily dosages of marijuana, but two able-bodied misfits like us could make fifty dollars a day easy.

≈ ≈ ≈ ≈ ≈ ≈ ≈

The constable stared at me in the rear-view mirror as he drove into the underground parking garage at the jail. It was a little spooky, going down there. The sun licked the back of my neck, and I knew I wouldn't feel that warmth for a while.

"You planning on a long stay?" the cop asked me.

"No, why would you say that?" I responded.

"You got on four shirts, *asshole*. Don't be a smart ass."

"Sorry," I said. "I don't know how long I'm staying, but I know it's cold in there."

"Here?"

"No, at Tucker," I replied.

"Yeah. But at least you know what's coming. It's better to get these things over with on your own terms."

My own terms would have been with a lawyer who could get the charges dropped, but what the hell. I agreed that it was good to get this over with.

Once inside, I believe I was treated a little better than my previous visits, but that could have just been the weed talking. They still made me undress, *completely*, and they still made me bend over and cough while a guard stared up my backside. They took my shoestrings and belt from me and allowed me to put back on all of my other clothes once I shook them out and proved there were no drugs or weapons concealed.

After that they took me to a holding cell. There were six people already in there. Two of them were balled into a fetal position in opposite corners. Everyone gave me a once over when I entered, but there were no prolonged stares.

There were no chairs, benches, or any other type of furniture in that holding cell. So if you wanted to sit or lie down, the floor was your only option. In a far corner, there were two stalls with no doors. The toilets inside were metal with no seats, and they had a sink connected to the back of them. That's right, folks; you had to shit, wash your hands, and get drinking water from the same stinky contraption.

I found an empty spot on the floor and sat quietly.

PLAN C (AND MORE KWB SHORTS)

There were no watches allowed in the holding cells and no clocks around. So from that point on, it was hard to get a good estimate of time. The room I was in could conceivably hold fifty men, but we never had more than fifteen. We got new inmates at a rate of about seven per hour, and inmates were called out of our tank to be arraigned at approximately the same pace.

Every now and then someone would ask the newest guy what time it was when he got arrested. This was the best we could do as far as knowing what hour it was. By the time I was arraigned, I had spent more than three hours in the holding tank. My high had worn off, I was getting sleepy, and I was hungry. They called me out with five other guys, and I was already hoping I could get off with some type of payment plan or community service.

They took us to a "court room," where an annoyed woman talked to us on television, rather than face to face. I stared up at a video monitor and listened intently as the judge read my rap-sheet. She was middle-aged and wily like Judge Judy, except she was black and overweight. The guy arraigned before me had been arrested for some type of violent and bloody assault, but she still set his bail pretty low, so I thought my mere traffic tickets would put me in the free-ride line. No such luck.

"Mr. Harris, are you aware that one of your citations was issued in 2008?"

"Yes, Your Honor," I said. "I had that one on a payment plan, but–"

"And you've got *five* no-insurance tickets from 2010."

"I think I had those on a payment plan, too," I lied.

"No, you had those set up for community service. It looks like you only went twice, so they went back to warrants. And you've got six more tickets here... You already plead guilty on four of them. What about these last two; the no registration and no inspection sticker from December last year?"

"I'm guilty on those, too," I said.

She scribbled something and shuffled papers. "Do you have a *job*, Mr. Harris?" The judge sounded like she knew damned well I didn't have a job.

"No."

"Well, it looks like you've got $3,500 worth of tickets, fines and court costs."

"I'd like to set those up for community service," I said seriously.

"Mr. Harris, you've had plenty of time to take care of this."

"I'd really like one more chance, Your Honor." There was a snicker from somewhere behind me.

"Mr. Harris, I am going to help you take care of this," she said as she wrote in my file. "Eight days in jail."

"You honor, I–" I took an ill-advised step forward. A guard approached quickly and pushed me back in line firmly. I didn't know why he was being so touchy. What was I going to do, attack the television screen?

"*Eight days,*" the judge said again and then looked up from her papers. "Once you get out, you're free and clear. It's good to go ahead and get this over with..."

"*Ugh,*" I hummed under my breath. I did not want to hear that shit again.

≈ ≈ ≈ ≈ ≈ ≈

After arraignment the guard took me to a holding cell. It was different than the one before, but the layout was the same. I was starting to feel claustrophobic when those doors slammed shut behind me. Anything could happen in those cells. The place was ugly, and nothing I smelled could be considered remotely pleasant.

I picked an empty spot on the floor and tried to get comfortable again. I took my sweater off, and it made an excellent pillow. I never fully slept, but I wasn't really awake when they finally called my name many hours later. I stood on tingly legs and allowed them to cuff my wrists again.

Eight of us were led out of the cell, down a hallway, and finally outside to a van. They stuffed me next to a burly, bearded guy who smelled like gasoline. We sat so close, our thighs touched from hip to knee. On my other side a skinny, skittish kid bit at his bottom lip but said nothing.

We all knew where we were going and what to expect, so there was little talk during the forty-five minute drive. It was completely dark by then, and to our dismay, the driver played country-western music the whole way.

PLAN C (AND MORE KWB SHORTS)

Tucker County Jail had holding cells that appeared to be designed by the same architect of the Overbrook Meadows facility. There were at least thirty bodies in the tank when they opened it up to let us in. It was dinnertime, but it wasn't loud or busy. Everyone shivered in their tee-shirts.

After our phone calls, the guards marched us to our actual unit, and this is where my story really begins. This unit is where I would spend the next eight days of my life, where I would gain twelve pounds, and where I would meet Tremont Grant.

I don't want to get too sentimental with this: I was a loser going into jail, a loser coming out, and to date I haven't done anything special to alter the track of mankind. But I did leave Tucker County a new person, and Tremont had a lot to do with that.

≈≈≈≈≈≈≈

My first night went horribly, just as expected. The unit they took us to had three cells. It didn't seem like the guards cared about who went to which cell. They just wanted us in bed. Carrying our mats, blankets, towels, and toiletries, we marched forward like we were in boot camp. We were like disciplined soldiers. The façade fell through when one of the Mexican fellows saw that he was being directed to a majority black cell.

"No. No, I no go there. I go *there*." He pointed towards the cell he preferred.

I don't know if the guard was always an asshole, or if he wanted to show out a little, but he was very pointed and acidic with his response.

"Hey! Hey! Listen, *Paco*, I don't know who the fuck you think you are, but you're getting in that goddamned cell!"

Not wanting to confront the guard, Paco turned and quickly caught up with another Hispanic inmate headed towards the favored cell. He grabbed the 2nd guy's shoulder and pleaded his case.

"Hey, *I* go here. You go there. We switch?"

I'm not sure if it was the idea of switching or the hand on the shoulder that set him off, but the 2nd guy was emphatically against the idea. He dropped his things and swung like he wanted to take Paco's head off. Paco took the blow to his temple and hit the ground, but he must have had springs in his ass, because he was up and punching in a split second.

The fight woke the unit up more than the lights would have. People jumped out of their bunks and ran to the bars, but no one left their cell even though the doors were open.

The guard who instigated the madness walked forward to separate the men. The other guard got on the radio and blurted out a code. Neither guard reacted as if this was a dire emergency.

"Everyone stay back!" one of them barked. "Stay in your cells! You, get over there! Get over by that bench!"

I hadn't been on my unit for one minute, and I was already being yelled at. My heart felt like it was trying to crawl out of my throat. My mouth was as dry as cotton. The guards directed me and the five other new guys to a neutral corner. We stood there obediently.

The fight didn't last long. The two guards were able to subdue the men without backup. Paco came up looking like he'd taken a sustained beating from bell to bell. The winner tried to shake off the guard holding him and proceed to the cell he wanted.

"Stop! What are you doing?" they shouted at him.

"I'm going to my cell," the dominant one said. He had a deep accent but spoke perfect English.

"You're not going anywhere. Get your ass down! Get on the ground!"

The inmate complied, and the melee was officially over. But the tremors would shake the unit for days. Four more guards finally rushed in, and they took the two fighters out roughly even though they were totally compliant by then.

Of the five new inmates left, I was white, there was another Hispanic man and three black men. The guards assigned us to our cells rather than let us pick. I got stuffed in the middle cell. Two of the black guys were assigned to the cell on the left, and the other two inmates got the Hispanic cell.

After we were all locked down for the night, another guard came in and cleaned up the mess left by the fighters. I watched him from my bunk with wide, frightful eyes.

I lie awake most of the night listening to strange men breathe and smelling things that should be banned. I did not sleep much the first day, and when I did, I dreamt about tornados for some reason.

PLAN C (AND MORE KWB SHORTS)

≈≈≈≈≈≈

The next morning we were awakened at six-thirty for the breakfast call. There was a clock on the wall in this unit, so we would always know what time it was and when our next meal would arrive. Mealtimes would come to govern our days.

No one talked much about the fight. The Mexicans were a tad more edgy than the rest of us, but they spoke mainly in Spanish. I suppose I could understand why a Mexican would want to be in a cell with his people, but I didn't understand why the fighters were so set against going into an all black cell. I would find out later, though. In the days to come, I would find out plenty.

I met Tremont at breakfast, but we didn't talk then. He stood in the chow line a few people ahead of me with his arms inside of his shirt and two big fists sticking out of the bottom. He was thin, a foot shorter than me. His skin was nearly as dark as charcoal.

Tremont was the exact picture that comes to mind when you hear about a rise in gang violence. His face would appear in your head when you heard about some old lady who got beat up for her purse on the bad part of town. Tremont had big lips, a shaved head and beady, shifty eyes. He was young, only eighteen. He barely managed a couple of hairs under his nose, but he was old enough for the blue wristband he sported.

I found out in the holding tank that every inmate at the jail had a different color wristband; depending on what their offense was. The blue ones were for those unlucky saps charged with felonies. I wore a yellow band. Red bands were for murder suspects, but luckily I didn't see any of them on my unit. I did see a few green bands, and I was eager to find out what those were about.

After breakfast everyone headed back to their cells, and I followed suit. One of my cellmates, a short, scruffy fellow named *Two Forty Shorty* (of all things) told me the cells were locked again after breakfast, and they would remain locked until lunch time. After lunch they would let us stay out until dinnertime, and after dinner the cells would remain open until lights out. I wasn't sleepy, but it was cold, and it felt good to get back in bed.

The blanket they gave us sucked royally, and I actually started feeling sorry for my cellies. Shorty showed me that you could tuck your shoes under your mattress and use the lump for a pillow, and I gave him one of my tee-shirts as gratitude for the tip. With the cells locked, there was nothing to do but talk, except no one was talking after breakfast.

Thirty minutes into our nap, a guard came over the intercom and instructed Ignacio Morales to *pack it up*. The inmate took his blanket and his mat to the guard station at the front of the unit, and then he disappeared through the same door they delivered our food through three times a day. But Ignacio didn't look as happy as I would have if they called my name. Tucker Jail had the most boring downtime I've ever experienced. We had no books and no television. We didn't even have a window through which we could watch the world pass us by.

≈ ≈ ≈ ≈ ≈ ≈

Lunchtime is when our unit finally woke up. I met Tremont after devouring a hamburger, a small bag of chips, a handful of carrot sticks and a grade-school size container of milk. I hadn't eaten raw carrot sticks in a while. I didn't remember liking them, but these were quite delectable. A few guys wouldn't touch their carrots. I watched them throw them away that morning, but in later days, I would capitalize and have a potato chip bag full of carrots in my bunk.

After eating, I sat on the bench and studied my surroundings for the first time. There were twenty men on our unit. Only four of us were white. Shorty, myself, and the fat guy who slept above me were all in the same cell, and I think this was a coincidence. The Mexicans having nearly a whole cell to themselves was fishy, and the third cell being all black was definitely not accidental.

There was a lot of graffiti on the benches and walls, but I didn't see any writing utensils lying around. We had three toilets and two showers but no stalls or shower curtains. If you took a shower, your goodies were going to be exposed. But no one sat there and stared at you. I washed up in the sink, as did most of the inmates, without ever getting totally naked during my stay.

PLAN C (AND MORE KWB SHORTS)

Tremont was using one of the payphones next to the bench where I sat. He was loud and obnoxious. I could hear his whole conversation. He wanted someone named Punkin to use her three-way calling to get another party on the line. Punkin must have told him that the phone would disconnect if she attempted the maneuver. Tremont told her to shut the fuck up and do what he said. Punkin knew what she was talking about, because a moment later the phone went dead in Tremont's ear. He slammed it down forcefully.

When he looked over and saw that I was watching him, I thought he would unleash his frustration on the skinny white kid, but he made conversation instead.

He sat across from me and asked, "Say, dog, you ever know a bitch so stupid?"

I was guarded, but I responded, "If you think about it, all girls are stupid – except our mamas. They're good people."

He stared at me for an awkward moment before smiling. "You got hold of your peeps yet?" he asked me.

"I don't have anyone to call," I admitted. "My mom's the one who turned me in, so I know she ain't coming to get me!"

He laughed. "For real?"

"Yeah, I'm serious. She called me and told me that she sent the constable over to my house when they came looking for me. They didn't even have my real address. I was tripping, but she said I needed to get it over with. I guess she was right. At least I had time to get ready."

"How you get ready?"

"I put on what I wanted."

He looked over my outfit. "And you chose that shit?" This cracked him up.

"Yeah. You're laughing, but I'm warm. I seen you over there shivering. I look stupid, but we're in jail. Everybody looks stupid."

Tremont nodded. "Yeah, you right, nigga. You right. If I had a chance to put on some more clothes, I damned sure would have. They got me in this bitch wearing shorts and this little-ass tee shirt."

I shook my head but didn't get too carried away with sympathy, lest he want my other tee shirt. Tremont had big teeth that were nice and white. They glistened when he smiled.

"So you just got some tickets, huh?" he asked.

"Yeah."

"They already told you how much time you got to do?"

"The judge said eight days."

"Nigga, that ain't shit," Tremont said. "You know who gon' be in this motherfucker acting a fool in a couple of days?"

"Who?" I asked, and I really wanted to know.

"Us motherfuckers with these blue tags on our arm." Tremont tugged at his wrist band. "Them with the reds, the greens; it's gon' be them motherfuckers trying to get out this bitch. We gon' go crazy if we can't find nobody to bond us out."

I nodded. "What's the green for?"

"They done violated they parole. They gon' be looking the sickest."

"What're you in for?" I asked him.

"Me? I got a dope case," Tremont said nonchalantly. "Judge gimme fifteen-thousand dollar bond. I can get out with fifteen hundred, if I can get in touch with my homeboy's mama. She got a block on her phone though, so I can't call over there. But I'ma get in touch with her in a minute. I got *too* many niggas out there. Fifteen-hundred ain't shit."

"How long you been here?" I asked him.

"Just got in last night," he said. "I seen you when you came in. You was with them Mexicans that was fighting, huh?"

"Yeah."

"Yeah, you was looking like a scared motherfucker! Your eyes was big as moon pies! I told my nigga, '*Look at Opie Taylor over there finna have a heart attack!*' Ha, ha. Nigga, you had me cracking up. I told my nigga I was gonna holler at you today. See what up with you."

"Why?" I asked him.

"'Cause. You look like the kinda dude who ain't gon' make it in this bitch. You ain't did nothing bad like what these dudes up in here did. This ain't for you," he said.

"What are you saying?" I asked him, starting to suspect a rat. "You gonna help me out in here?"

"I ain't gonna fight for you or nothing like that," Tremont said. "If you get caught up in some shit, I may try to holler at somebody for you. But if you gotta knuckle up, you gotta handle that yourself. You know how to fight?"

"Yeah," I said, though I'd never thrown a punch at anyone but my little brother. I'd never swung at anyone's head at all.

"Good," Tremont said. "I was in Golden Gloves for a minute. Coulda went all the way with that shit, ya hear me? I'm nice with these." He held up his battered fists. "I should be on TV like Mayweather. Shit got fucked up though," he trailed off. His eyes went unfocused for a moment as he sought a distant memory, perhaps.

"Why didn't that guy want to go in your cell?" I asked him.

"'Cause he *Mexican* and we *black*. That's it. We wouldn't have fucked with him or nothing, but Mexicans like that don't feel safe if they not with they own kind. Same in prison. Nah, it's *worse* in prison. In prison, it be all black, all white, and all Mexican. You won't see no blacks kicking it with Mexicans in prison. They take that shit real serious in there. Jail is like a little prison, though. You can kick it with a Mexican or black person in jail, but not in the pen."

Tremont stood abruptly. "I'm still sleepy, man. Finna lay it down, prolly 'til dinner." He yawned noisily. "But you good, though. Them eight days gon' fly by, watch. Least you know when you getting out. Most of us, we don't know if today's our last day, tomorrow, if we gotta stay here 'til we go to trial, or what..."

He tromped off to his cell holding his shorts up as he stepped. He seemed innocent enough, but I had mixed feelings about him. My father had no understanding or tolerance for people like Tremont. I don't know if I could say my dad was completely racist – he didn't have anything against black people in general – but he definitely didn't care much for the young, gangbanger types.

I didn't harbor any of the hate my father tried to pass down, but I couldn't deny the validity of his thinking. Tremont probably did not complete school, and he sold crack to his own people. If cocaine could make a millionaire like Whitney Houston destroy her legacy, how much more devastating was it for poor people?

When you're in jail, there's a lot of time to contemplate such things.

≈≈≈≈≈≈≈

I sat on the bench after lunch doing absolutely nothing for a whole hour. Half of the unit slept. Others milled around. A group of Mexicans talked jovially at one of the other benches. One guy was taking a shower, and another was doing pushups. Three more inmates were crowded around the payphones, trying to get information about their lawyers, their bonds, and their charges.

You'd be exposed to a myriad of emotions around those phones, so I made my way to the guy working out to see if I could get some type of workout regimen started. He was happy to oblige.

His name was Kevin Whitmore, and he was so fit, I never would've guessed he was forty-five years old. Whitmore was the color of cherry wood. He was bald, and he wore a pair of horn-rimmed glasses that had been taped on both arms.

He greeted me with a hearty handshake, and I noticed the green wristband on his arm.

"What you in for?" he asked me.

"Tickets," I said.

"I got a parole violation," Whitmore said. Between pushups he told me, "I got sent to prison ten years ago for trying to kill my wife. We got back together when I was locked up, and she took me back in when I got paroled. Then I found out she was letting damned near every man in the neighborhood skeet all over her while I was locked up. I got a right to beat her ass for that, don't I?"

I shrugged. "Uh, I don't know."

"The answer is, '*No,*'" Whitmore said with a wink. "Or else my black ass wouldn't be locked up again."

"How do you stay in such good shape?" I asked him as a distraction.

"Got me a personal trainer certificate when I was locked up in Greensboro," my new friend told me. "I thought I could get a job at one of those fitness centers when I got out, but they were acting shady because I been to prison. They basically told me my certificate wasn't worth shit."

"It's obviously worth something," I said, trying not to sound gay as I checked out his physique. "I don't think you have any body fat at all."

Whitmore smiled. "You want me to show you how to work out in here? We ain't got shit else to do. Might as well stay fit."

I nodded eagerly. "Yeah, that would be cool."

Whitmore told me he could work out every muscle on his body without weights, and he could produce noticeable definition with simple objects like a bunk bed, a chair, or the bench we ate lunch on. He demonstrated six or seven workout techniques, and I was completely awed by the time we stopped for the day. Whitmore said we could workout more after supper if I wanted to, but my muscles felt like I received tetanus shots all over my body.

It was only three o'clock by then; still a few hours before dinner. I was not through my first full day at the jail, but I was already bored out of my mind. This had to be the worst place imaginable. I know I broke a law (well, several laws), and I was cool with doing my time, but I thought they should offer *something* for the inmates to do. I would have read the Bible from cover to cover at that point. With no other options, I got in my bunk and lie on my back. I stared up at the ceiling and had not dozed when the dinner call finally came.

≈ ≈ ≈ ≈ ≈ ≈ ≈

Tremont jumped on one of the two phones right after dinner and stayed on it for at least an hour. I didn't eavesdrop, but unless you whispered, anyone near the benches could hear your conversation. I don't think Tremont knew how to whisper. Well slept and well fed, Tremont wanted only one thing: Somebody needed to bond him the fuck out. I watched as he pleaded with several people.

He tried being cordial: "Say, Blood, I got popped on *another* fucking dope charge. Yeah. Yeah, I know. You know a nigga *sick* up in here. Naw, ain't no problem like that, I just need to get *outta here*, ya dig? Need to get some money to get me a lawyer."

He tried guilt: "Say, check this out: You remember when you did them five years down in Leavenworth? I know I ain't never come see you, nigga, but who sent you something every week? Who got you that radio you wanted? Who got you them new socks and drawers? C'mon, pimpin', you need to get with J-Rock and them and get some money together for a nigga."

He tried sympathy: "Mama I didn't do nothing this time! You know how they is over there. The laws roll up, and *everybody out there* going to jail. I was just chilling, Mama – *swear to God.* If you help me out, I'll be cool. For real. We can go to church and everything."

Finally, he tried aggression: "Bitch, I ain't call to talk to your ho ass anyway! Put Rock on the goddamned phone! Where the fuck he at? When he get there you need to – naw, *bitch*, you listen to what the fuck I'm saying! You know what, when I get out this motherfucker, I'ma fuck yo– You heard what the fuck I said? You hear me? *Bitch*?"

Tremont slammed the phone down. This was a jailhouse phone, so none of the parts were detachable. Everything on it looked to be reinforced, but I still expected to see the damned phone shatter before I left the unit.

Flustered, Tremont came and sat down across from me with a glare that could melt paint off the wall. There was only one moment during my eight days in jail that I felt real, live *fear*, and this was that occasion.

His face was frozen in a sneer. I didn't know what to say, but I knew something should be said.

"That same stupid girl?" I asked.

He nodded. "Yeah, man. I don't know what this ho thinking. I got my dope house on Jessamine, right? She come over there damn near every day. We ain't never had no problem before – me and her, ya dig? She my homeboy's girl, but I takes care of her. She do that brown, you know? She likes to get her nose dirty. She get a little from me sometimes. Now she acting like I ain't never getting out of here. You know how they do you; out of sight, out of mind."

"When we get out of here, I'll help you find her," I joked. "We can kidnap her, throw her off a bridge."

Tremont smiled. "You ever kill somebody, white boy?"

"Why do y'all do that?" I asked.

"Do what?"

"Call me '*white boy.*'"

"What you mean?" Tremont asked. "You *is* white."

"Yeah, I'm white, but you know what I mean. Whenever y'all meet a white person, you call him '*white boy.*' I got an uncle who even had that tattooed on his arm when he was in the pen. In big, black letters it just says, 'WHITE BOY.' I don't get it."

"Well," Tremont leaned forward with his forearms on the table, "your uncle prolly got into some white, Aryan Nation type of gang when he got locked up. In the pen, it ain't bad to call a white person 'white boy.' They call each other that. They take it like it's they pride or something. As far as me, why I do it..." He shrugged. "I don't know. I guess the same reason you call us *'you people.'*"

"I didn't say *'you people.'*"

"Naw, you said 'Why do *y'all* call us white boy,' but that's the same as saying 'Why do *you people* call us white boy?' See, you didn't ask why *I* do it, you said *'y'all,'* so you asking about my whole race just 'cause of something I did. That's stereotyping, bruh."

I was taken aback. "That's deep, man. I never thought about it like that. I gotta watch what I say, I guess."

"Hmph. Not me, man," Tremont said. "What you say don't really matter much as what you *do* in this world. You can say whatever you want to hurt somebody, but it's not gon' hurt as much as if you crack they head open."

There was no arguing that. "Damn, you're like Socrates," I told him.

"Yeah. Wish I had a blunt. I could smoke you out and tell you some stuff."

"First of all," I informed him, "you would *get* smoked out. Nobody smokes more weed than me. Second, I'm bored as hell in here, so you can tell me whatever you want. Just as long as we're not reminiscing about weed and cigarettes. I want a cigi so bad right now..."

"That'll wear off in a couple of days." Tremont looked around. "You wanna play bones or something?"

"You got dominoes in here?" Tremont was full of wonders.

"One of them niggas in there got some." He shot a thumb in the direction of his cell. "They jacked up, but they'll do. You can make some more, though. Don't nobody in your cell got none?"

"How are we supposed to get them?" I asked. "Does someone have to mail them to us, or something?"

Tremont laughed. "Naw, Blood, you gotta make 'em yourself!"

"How the hell do you make dominoes?"

He shook his head. "Damn, nigga. You ain't been locked up before?"

"Just overnight a couple of times," I admitted.

"What's your name?"

"I'm Wes."

"Well, Wes, I'm Tremont. Come over to my house, and let me show you what the damn deal."

And I did.

Tremont showed me how to make dominoes in jail, which is the same technique used to make playing cards. First you have to save up milk cartons from the meals. Once you rinse and dry them off, you cut away the four sides.

When you get enough squares from the milk cartons, you have to go to the guard station up front and tell them you want to fly a kite to the nurse or the jail's supervisor. He will give you a small form to fill out and a little pencil with no metal or eraser. The form is trash. The pencil is what you want.

Now you can fill out the dots on your dominoes or draw your cards. The guards don't care about the kite. They know you only wanted the pencil half the time. These are the same pencils used to make all of the graffiti I saw on the tables and walls when I first came in.

I stayed in Tremont's cell for hours. I met all of his bunkmates, and I have to say I've never seen so many innocent people in one place in my life. A tall guy named Stacy swore the police pulled him over in a Jeep he just purchased, and they took him straight to jail because he had not validated the registration yet. A short, pudgy gentleman named Buck said he was merely *verbally* arguing with his girlfriend when the police busted-in, pushing and shoving and hand-cuffing (only him). Calvin was trying to pawn a lawn mower that definitely was *not* stolen. Junior did not own or throw the gun the cops pinned on him. And Desmond was just standing on the corner waiting for a bus when he got arrested. The other two guys didn't tell me their offenses. I didn't know Texas had turned into a police state, but that was the clear consensus.

≈ ≈ ≈ ≈ ≈ ≈

When the guards announced it was time to lock down for the night, I left Tremont's cell in good spirits. Tremont's cellmates did not seem to accept me like Tremont did, but they weren't rude to me. They might not have liked me, but they didn't *dis*like me, that much was clear. Their homemade dominoes were decent, but no one on the unit had attempted to make a deck of cards. This was going to be my new project.

Sleep was elusive, but no one slept immediately after lights out. Tremont's cell did not sleep at all. They laughed loudly as they recanted their tales from the hood. They talked about famous women they liked. They debated who the best rapper was and began to rap their favorite songs.

At three o'clock in the morning, Tremont's cell was still going strong, much to the chagrin of most of the other inmates. A few people in my cell tossed and turned and muttered under their breath about how they wished the blacks would shut the hell up. But no one said anything loud enough for Tremont's cell to hear them.

At breakfast time, Tremont and his crew staggered out of their cells groggily and ate quietly. They slept after breakfast, and they slept after lunch, too. This was their routine. Tremont said they stayed up all night on purpose so they wouldn't have to be awake during the boring parts of the day. I asked him if he knew they were keeping everyone else up all night, and he said, "Fuck 'em. Bet nobody won't say shit about it." And no one did, for awhile.

≈ ≈ ≈ ≈ ≈ ≈

After my first day, time started to go by a little quicker. My schedule was simple, my hobby was engrossing, and I was eating better than I had since I moved out of my mom's house. I've heard a lot of bad stuff about the lack of respect from correctional officers and the food quality in jail, but none of that was relevant at Tucker.

Every day, after breakfast usually, the guard would come over the intercom and tell someone else to *pack it up*. And every day, usually after lunch, we would get new prisoners on our unit. The black cell always stayed black, and the Mexican cell remained fully Mexican. My cell was still the neutral one, for whatever reason.

The guy above me got bonded out on my second day, and I took his top bunk. I worked out with Whitmore until he got transferred, and I continued my daily exercises without him. I talked to Tremont everyday but never moved into his cell. I wanted to go, but I never got an invite.

Two Forty Shorty got released on my third day. I really didn't want to see him go. He was the only person I talked to in my cell. Shorty was good at tearing cardboard and had made half of my playing cards. I asked him where he lived, thinking we might hook up when I got out. But Shorty lived at a homeless shelter, and he couldn't guarantee he'd be there on any given date.

Before he left, I finally asked about his name. Shorty admitted that he was a no good bastard with a heavy drug habit. He said he tried to work every day, and he would spend his daily wages on dope and beer. He would get two forty ounces of Old English every evening from the same corner store. He got his nickname from the guys who hung out around the store.

Tremont was the only person in there I considered a friend. Day after day I watched the progress of his case with empathy. He had been counting on his friend J Rock to bail him out, but J Rock got arrested himself two days into our stay. Tremont's other friends from the hood were not as reliable. First he heard that someone had paid his bail, and then he heard that it wasn't paid at all. Later he was told that there was some kind of hold-up on his bond. Tremont had a lawyer appointed to him by the courts, but he was still waiting to hear from him.

"You know something," he told me one day after lunch, "this system's set up to keep a motherfucker like me down."

I felt close enough to him to ask, "How you mean? Seems like everybody can do whatever they want in life. Whatever happens is pretty much what you make of it."

Tremont nodded. "Mmm, hmm. See, that's exactly what they *want* you to think. Young white boys like you; you're the one this country is for. As long as you keep thinking people like me choose our fates, you won't do nothing to change it when you get older. You'll decide you like things just the way they are, and everything will stay *just like it is.*"

"Are you saying you don't have the same chances everybody else has, the same chances I have?"

He shook his head. "You see it like that 'cause you was raised to see it like that. You see what they show you on TV. *MTV*. You see those rappers getting rich. Will Smith, Oprah Winfrey. They good, but do you know how many niggas it is between them? For every Beyonce, you got ten thousand niggas who ain't never gon' own they own house or car.

"This here," Tremont waved his arm around the room, "this here ain't for people like you, people with skin like you got. This here is for *us*." He shot a thumb towards his cell. "It's for niggas and Mexicans. Niggas on my block know the damned deal. Them judges is passing out football numbers like they candy or something."

"What do you mean?" I asked.

"I mean niggas know we getting *dealt with* in them courts. Them judges ain't playing no more."

"No, *'football numbers.'* What's that?"

"That's what they giving young niggas like me nowadays," Tremont explained. "You used to could get popped with a gun and some crack, and they'll give you like two years, or two to five. Now, they giving *football numbers*. That's like, center and linebacker numbers, you know what I'm saying? Niggas is getting *hard time*, up to like forty or fifty years nowadays. Lock 'em up, throw the fucking key *away*. Don't have to worry about 'em no more."

"You think the system is set up to do that?"

"I know it is. These motherfuckers out to get us."

"I mean, do you think you can't do nothing *but* go to jail? Just because you're black, you have to go to jail?"

"Let me ask you a question, Shaggy. Or even better, let me put it to you this way: You got your *A*, your *B*, and your *C*. Alright?" He assigned each of these letters to one of his fingers. "Alright, so *A* is the fact that niggas was slaves. Ain't no disputing that, right?"

"Right," I said. "Nig–, I mean, black people were slaves."

He grinned at my almost-faux pas. "Alright, so *B*, the slaves got free, right?"

I nodded.

"Cool," Tremont said. "So check this out: Your *C* is the fact that niggas is doing bad than a motherfucker right now. Huh? Niggas is doing bad today, right?"

"Well, yeah. Some black people are doing bad today," I acknowledged.

"Yeah," Tremont said, as if he'd just tricked me. "So you got your *A*, *B*, and *C*. *A* was fucked up, *B* was cool, but *C* is fucked up, so what's the problem?"

"*C*?" I asked.

"Naw, not just *C*. *A* is fucked up, too, ya dig? Us being slaves was fucked up. Maybe not fucked up like today, but still, *A* and *C* are both fucked up. What's the real problem?" he asked again.

I didn't know I was going to school that day, and I didn't have an answer.

"*B* was fucked up, too!" Tremont declared. "Something must have been wrong with *B* or *C* wouldn't be fucked up. They freed the slaves, but they couldn't make them motherfuckers who been hanging us, they couldn't make them all of a sudden start liking us the next day. We never got no 40 acres and no mule, so we had to start out with shit. And now a bunch of us are still in that same shit."

"You're saying blacks are messed up today because of slavery?" I asked.

"I'm saying just what I said, young buck. We was slaves. They set us free. Now we fucked up today. I can't figure everything out, but I can see them three things right there. They freed the slaves in Lincoln's day, but we was still riding in the back of the bus in Kennedy's day. So plan *B* had to be fucked up. They fucked up plan *B*, and we still fucked up today. So, you tell me what the system wants from us."

I was totally dumbfounded. "Tremont, dude, how you know so much?"

"Damn, *Blood*, you think I didn't *never* go to no school, or what?"

"Yeah, but, I went to school, too. They didn't tell me all of that stuff."

Tremont smiled. "Now you coming along, dog. It's like I told you; you think how you think 'cause you was raised to think like that. In school, they teach you what *white folks* did. You ain't gon' find out what black folks did in no school. You gotta read on your own for that. Watch shit on TV – not no bullshit, but some real shit, like Malcolm X. Watch some black and white documentaries. Channel 13 got some good stuff, but you only catch it in February. But as far as that *A, B, C* shit, I come up with that on my own."

I still couldn't believe the things he'd just told me. "Tremont, you're like, man... I don't know what to say."

"Oh, brothers will surprise your ass every now and then." He smiled. "You see a nigga on the streets and be like, '*That nigga don't know shit.*' But every now and again, a nigga will surprise you by what he know."

Knowing what's going on but still powerless to stop it, I thought.

I took a lot of what he said to my cell that night and rolled it around in my head until I started thinking reparations was a good idea. Tremont was deep, I had to give him that. He may not have been book smart, but he knew the fundamentals of life. He had common sense and street smarts, and his A,B,C theory made more sense than any conversation I ever heard about the repercussions of slavery.

I didn't sleep well that night, and it wasn't entirely the noise or the smells or my threadbare mat this time.

≈≈≈≈≈≈≈

Tremont didn't lose it until the day before my release. I suppose I knew it was coming; all of that tension coiling in him like a python. I was still caught completely off guard, however. I was eating lunch, sitting no more than three feet away from him when it happened. Tremont was on the phone, getting nowhere with his case as usual. A new inmate, a tall and dark-skinned thug who bunked with the Mexicans, approached and sat next to me for a moment. I was totally into my meal, and he wasn't bringing any leftovers, so I didn't give him a second thought.

After a minute the new guy stood and tried to use the phone next to Tremont. It must have been malfunctioning, because he slammed it down and said, "Say, you need to get off the phone, nigga."

112

I didn't believe he was serious, but when I looked up he was standing chest to chest with Tremont. They were close enough to smell each other's breath, but Tremont didn't seem upset, so I went on eating.

Tremont casually told whoever he was talking to, "Say, let me call you back." He hung up the phone, took a step away from the man, and then he spun quickly and delivered two precise blows to the inmate's head. The first punch was an excellent straight right to the jaw that probably did the trick. The second strike was a stiff left that caught the poor bastard squarely on his forehead. The two blows were so swift, it looked like Tremont had done nothing more than shrug his shoulders.

The new guy leaned towards the bench as if he was going to sit next to me again, but he continued sliding until he was lying flat on his back. It was a slow fall, as if someone had pricked and deflated him. A bruise sprouted and swelled on his jaw, and I saw that his forehead was split open like a cantaloupe. My mouth fell open. I turned wide-eyed to the guard station and saw that it was occupied, but as usual the guard was looking in the other direction. Tremont looked around at the other inmates, and then he looked at me. Without a word he went into his cell as if he'd done no more than share pleasantries with the victim.

Not sure what to do, I continued my meal with shaky fingers as others came to inspect the body. I didn't know what to think. The guy wasn't moving. His chest rose and fell, so I knew he wasn't dead, but the wound on his forehead looked like the exit hole of some massive firearm. The cut went from his hairline to the bridge of his nose and had spread more than half an inch at the center. Blood snaked down his face in bright red rivulets that settled in his hair and ears.

The Mexicans came to check him out, but no one offered to help. They just wanted to get a look at him before they sauntered back to their bunks. The guys from Tremont's cell were the most animated. They came out and seemed jovial about the scene. One of them leaned over the body and screamed into the unconscious face: "You got knocked the *fuck* out, nigga!"

Others were more concerned about what the guards would do. The beaten man had to go to the infirmary, that much was certain, but what about Tremont? As soon as the body was discovered, the whole unit would be on lock-down; we would have to stay in our cells for the rest of the day, and it was only lunchtime.

Tremont's cellmates laughed and stepped over the body for a while before deciding it had to be moved. Not wanting to violate the Mexicans' space, two of them grabbed the defeated man by the ankles and dragged him into *my* cell.

I was spooked, but on some insane level I also found a bit of humor in the scene. I'd never seen anyone get knocked out like that outside of television. This was the real deal. He was seriously out-cold, and for what? Talking shit to someone he knew nothing about had garnished him a scar that would probably be visible for the rest of his life. I finished eating, and when the guards came to collect our trays, they did not see the body.

After lunch, Tremont and his crew hung out in their cell. I wanted to talk to him, but I didn't have the balls to go in there. I didn't know if Tremont's change was something that would affect me or not, and I wasn't going out of my way to find out.

Eventually I had no choice but to go into my own cell and talk with my cellmates about the predicament we were in. The overall understanding was that no one knew *nothing about nothing*. When the guy woke up, we wouldn't know what happened to him or how he got in our cell. And we definitely wouldn't talk to the guards. Oddly, no one felt pity for the man. They were curious about why Tremont *smashed-on* him, but mainly we just wanted him up and out of our cell.

A full hour after the assault, the bloodied inmate finally started moving again. He kicked out one leg and raised his arm a little. Thirty minutes after that, his eyes fluttered open. When he tried to make it to his feet, I saw a few of my cellmates laughing under their breath. I did feel sorry for him then, but other than snitching (which would put me in hot water but do nothing to stitch up his head), there was nothing I could do for him.

"You alright, man," I asked when he finally made it to a standing position.

"What happened?" His voice was slightly slurred.

Everyone said they didn't know. The bruised phone-jacker staggered around a bit before realizing his face was covered with blood. There were no mirrors on the unit, but we did have a square piece of sheet metal bolted to the wall that was shiny enough to offer some reflection. The guy took a gander and didn't like the look of his forehead at all.

"What the hell happened?" he asked again, but no answers were forthcoming.

Rather than leave our cell to investigate, he shuffled to the intercom button on our wall and summoned the guards.

"What do you want?" a voice came back.

"I need a doctor!" the inmate yelled.

Three officers came for him in less than thirty seconds. They asked him what happened. When he couldn't explain, they asked the whole unit. The Mexicans didn't know, and our cell didn't talk, either. Tremont's cell, still euphoric, laughed and offered their best explanation.

"He slipped on a tomato!"

"Fuck y'all, I didn't slip on no tomato!" the outcast yelled back. "One of them niggas stole on me," he told the guards, but they didn't investigate his claim. Instead they helped the inmate pack up his things. They led him off the unit and locked the rest of us down for an unspecified amount of time.

Tremont's cellmates teased the injured inmate on his way out, the most poignant criticism being: "Punk-ass, nigga! If you don't like it, bond out!"

I was glad this was the last night I had to spend in jail. There was a knot in my stomach and blood on my floor. Even worse, Tremont was never the same after this.

≈ ≈ ≈ ≈ ≈ ≈

On lock-down there was little to do but wait for dinner and discuss the day's events. Unless you're asleep, lock-down is not an ideal setting. As bad as it was already, you'd think it couldn't get any worse until they took away the few liberties you were allowed. You couldn't get to the lunch benches while on lock-down, so there was no working out or playing cards or dominoes. Plus everyone lost access to the telephones.

When dinner came, all eyes were on Tremont. Most of these eyes peeked around sandwiches and over milk cartons, but they all found Tremont. We were all capable of violence, but Tremont had proven himself not only able, but willing. His cellmates talked about the two-punch combo like he was Ali. And

115

because I was the best witness, I had to verify the accounts throughout the meal. Yes, it was true that Tremont split the guy's forehead open with one punch. Yes, Tremont did have the fastest hands I'd ever seen.

By the time our meal was over, Tremont was the official badass on our unit and had earned the respect and fear of all. I watched two people offer him the main course from their meal. After dinner, Tremont was allotted a wide berth at the pay phones. I did my workout for the day and was shuffling milk-carton-cards for a game of solitaire when Tremont sat across from me.

"Say, that was some fucked up shit happened earlier, huh?"

I agreed that it was.

"That wasn't really my fault, though. Nobody ain't supposed to talk to you like that. I was on the phone minding my own business. He came up to *me*. You saw him, didn't you? You saw him."

"Yeah, I don't know what he was thinking," I said.

"I been cool with everybody," Tremont said. "You know? I ain't been starting no shit. Right?"

I nodded. I couldn't believe it, but he was seeking my approval.

"This is jail," Tremont said. "Nigga come up to you, trying to check you like that, you gotta do what you gotta do, or niggas won't respect you. If I give up the phone like that, I might as well just hand the nigga my tray every time we eat."

I nodded. "So, what's gonna happen to you?" I asked. "Are you gonna get in trouble?"

"Naw. He didn't even know who hit him. If he would've stood there and said '*It was him right there,*' then, yeah, I guess a nigga could've got in trouble. But he didn't. It's too late now."

"What about everybody else?" I asked.

"What? You mean everybody who saw it?"

"Yeah."

"Shit, if they was gon' say something, they would've said it. Too late now. They can shoot a kite to the guards if they want, but they can't prove it. It's eight niggas in my cell. If all of us say we didn't do it, and the nigga who got stole-on don't know who did it, they ain't finna do shit to me just 'cause one of y'all motherfuckers tell on me."

I didn't like the way Tremont said, *y'all.*

He looked at me and smiled. "It's about to be your last day, ain't it?"

I couldn't help but return his smile. "Yeah. Today's it for me. Tomorrow they *gotta* let me outta here. What about you?" I regretted asking as soon as the words left my lips.

Tremont's smile faltered. "You know the deal, Blood. They try to act like a nigga don't know shit, ya know? I finally gets a hold of my lawyer, and he wants me to take a deal. Guess what they wanna give me for five dime rocks. No pistol. Not individually wrapped. Just five rocks. You could fit 'em all in one spoon. Guess how much."

I didn't want to guess.

"Thirty years," he said. "I'm eighteen. They wanna keep me 'til I'm fifty."

He paused to let this sink in.

"This is your first offense?" I asked.

"Naw. You only need three felonies, though. They get you with three felonies, and they can give you *life,* just like that. Three strikes, ya know. They got them judges up in there playing baseball." Tremont smiled, but his throat got caught on the word *baseball,* and I knew he was close to tears. I did not want him to cry in front of me. Maybe sensing it, he stood and yawned. He wiped his face and eyes as if just waking up.

"I'm finna go to the house. You gon' be out here a minute?"

It hurt me to hear him refer to that cell as his *house.* "Yeah, I'm gonna play a couple of games," I told him.

"Cool, cool. Gotta stay busy. I'ma be back in a minute to holler at you," he said, but he never came back out.

They locked us down for the night, and that was the last serious talk I had with Tremont. The pent up rage he meant to unleash on our unit, however, had only just begun.

≈ ≈ ≈ ≈ ≈ ≈ ≈

After lights out, I lie awake in my bunk anxious about getting out the next day. I had seen, smelled, and heard things during my stay that would occupy my mind for months and years to come. At midnight, Tremont's cell was as noisy as usual, and by three in the morning, even I was getting a little tired of their

117

nonstop chatter and singing. I'm sure others on our unit felt the same way, but no one was stupid enough to say anything, or so I thought.

Outlaw is one of my favorite Tupac songs. With an angry tone, the rapper croons about how much he hates the justice system. Tupac boasts about cursing out the prosecutor and shooting at the judge during his trial. When Tremont started rapping this song, everyone in his cell became excited and *loud*. Usually only one or two guys would remember all of the lyrics when they played their karaoke game, but for this one, all eight cellmates sang in unison. The racket was intense, but one voice screamed loudly enough to penetrate the banter.

"Could y'all shut the fuck up?!"

The words sliced through the unit like a knife, effectively (if only temporarily) creating a bubble of silence that was like the eye of a storm. My eyes popped open, and I sat up in bed like I heard a gunshot. I couldn't believe it. I didn't recognize the voice, but certain things were immediately clear: It came from the Mexicans' cell, it was Caucasian, and it was the voice of a dead man. Someone had walked into a lion's den wearing pork chop drawers. My heart thudded as if I was the offender.

"Who the fuck said that?"

No reply.

"Hey, who the fuck is that?"

"It's late." The stranger tried to sugar coat it. "I just want to go to sleep. You guys have been talking and yelling all night. We just want to sleep." He sought support, but no one co-signed for him.

For the next three hours, the new guy tried to shut up and disappear into his mattress, but Tremont's cell would not let up. Every person in cell number one threatened this still-unidentified person for the remainder of the night. How dare he tell them to shut the fuck up? Who did he think he was? They would get him as soon as the guards opened the cages for breakfast – that was a certainty. Did he have any idea what they were going to do to him?

By the time the cells opened at six, everyone was primed for the fight. We wanted to know who was stupid enough to bring this wrath upon themselves. It turned out to be a dopey, slack-jawed bumpkin who looked like he wrestled bears in his free time.

He was taller than me, six-five maybe, and weighed at least 260 pounds. He wore a large pair of jeans that had grass stains on the knees. His tee shirt was filthy, and it had creamy patches under the armpits. If I had to guess his name, I think *Cletus* fit him pretty well.

Still, he was the biggest guy on the unit. I thought that would give pause to the promised ass whooping, but Tremont stormed out of his cell and went straight for the yokel.

Cletus was the only white guy coming out of that cell, so there was no question about who had interrupted the singing last night. And despite giving up a hundred pounds, Tremont didn't show any fear for the man. He stomped up to him like a drill sergeant and stood before him defiantly.

"What was that shit you was talking last night?" Tremont barked.

Most of the inmates crowded around the two, but others, fearful of getting involved, got in line for their food as if nothing was out of the ordinary. There was only a one minute delay between the opening of our cells and the guards showing up to deliver our trays. I didn't think Tremont had time to fight the man that quickly. It was senseless. Did he want to get caught? Cletus had only yelled one thing, and to be honest, it was a decent request. I didn't know who I should feel sorrier for, but I watched the confrontation closely, as if I'd purchased pay-per-view seats.

"I just wanted to go to sleep," Cletus said. "I don't want no trouble." He tried to walk around the skinny gangsta, but Tremont side-stepped and cut him off. I looked up to the guard station. They were not there yet, but I could hear the cart rolling down the hallway.

"Naw, bitch, I want you to say what the fuck you said last night," Tremont dared. "You said, '*Shut the fuck up.*' I want you to say that shit now!"

"I just wanna—"

SMACK!

It was an open-handed slap that caught Cletus square on the cheek. A punch of similar caliber would have stumbled if not floored the man. But the slap was more vicious and disrespectful. Tremont had serious speed. There was no way to guard against the blow.

Cletus flinched. His eye teared-up on the impacted side, but other than that he didn't move. It was obvious the slap had hurt him, though. A big, red blotch, the exact shape of Tremont's hand and fingers, marred his skin like red paint.

"What? Do something, bitch!" Tremont balled his fist. "I dare you to do something!" Tremont's cellmates surrounded the new guy as if they would jump in, but Tremont shook his head slightly and they backed off. I looked to the guard station again and could see the officers rounding the corner. Twenty more paces and they would be at our unit.

"You's a ho!" Tremont berated him. "You's a ho, ain't ya? Ain't ya?!"

He accented his question with another **SMACK**!

Cletus raised an arm this time to ward off the blow, but it was too little, too late. The second slap hit the same spot. His whole face was beet red. A trickle of blood pooled in his nostril but didn't fall.

"You bet not *never* say shit to me again as long as you on this unit, punk! You hear me? *You hear me*?!"

Possibly fearing another strike, Cletus did the unthinkable. He took a shuddering breath, lowered his head and said, "Okay."

The two slaps were devastating enough, but that one word sealed Cletus' fate for the remainder of his stay in Tucker. There was nowhere he could go and nothing he could do to take it back. He was a defeated man, and all of the predators knew that he wouldn't fight back.

≈≈≈≈≈≈≈

After breakfast, they finally came over the intercom and said something I'd wanted to hear since my introduction to the unit: "*Wesley Harris, pack it up!*"

The smile that grew on my face was all-encompassing, deep and spiritual. Sometimes you don't feel the burden you're carrying until it's lifted from you. My heart was suddenly so light, I believe I could have floated from that building. Those eight days were like eight months, and I didn't feel like the same person anymore. I didn't know who I was or what I was going to do, but I knew that everything in my life was wrong, and it had been for a long time.

My cellmates wished me luck, scavenged my toiletries and told me they'd see me later. I promised them that they most certainly would *not* see me later as I walked out of my cell for the last time. Before stepping off of the unit, I stopped by Tremont's cell and dropped my mat and blanket.

"You out, huh? I told you it wasn't gon' be that long," he called from his bunk.

I stood there, unsure how to say what I felt. I didn't want to look foolish. I took off my sweater and took a healthy sniff. It didn't smell too bad.

"You want this?" I asked, holding it out to him.

Tremont jumped out of his bunk and met me at the bars. "I can have it?"

"Yeah, if you don't mind red."

He twisted his face. "Nigga, hell naw I don't mind red. You ain't seen my tats?" He exposed his forearms, but I didn't know what the markings meant. He clarified: "I'm a Blood, homey. Tate Street Pirus, ya know?"

I didn't think that was such a great honor, so I just said, "Oh."

I handed him the sweater through the bars, and he put it on immediately. "Damn, this shit is warm." He shook his head affectionately. "Man, you don't know what this means to a nigga."

I nodded. "Yeah, I do." I gathered my things and studied his face for a moment. I didn't think I'd ever see him again, but on the odd chance I did, I wanted to remember him.

"I don't wanna see you in here no more," Tremont said.

I told him he wouldn't.

I checked out of jail that morning with great expectations. I felt like Pip leaving London as a proper gentleman. The world was open, and it was big and beautiful. I made up my mind right then that I would never waste another precious day searching for comfort on a metal bunk or seeking recreation in milk carton dominoes.

EPILOGUE

PLAN C (AND MORE KWB SHORTS)

There's a kid I'm working with. He's supposed to be with me every day after school, but lately I've had to hunt him down. He lives at 1824 Jessamine Avenue. Whenever I search for him, I can't help but think about the dope house Tremont Grant told me he had on that street. I haven't seen Tremont in ten years, since I left Tucker County Jail, but I still think of him sometimes. I've repeated his *ABC* theory on more than one occasion.

The kid I'm looking for is named Anthony Mitchell. He's in the fifth grade, tall, athletic, and as cantankerous as a hooked catfish. Honestly, it's a wonder I've gained any progress with him. His mother is a self-admitted drug user, his two older brothers are in prison and his father was killed while Anthony was still in diapers. His grandmother raises him most of the time.

He was referred to me by the principal of his grade school. She was at her wits' end with the child. Thus far, neither detentions nor suspensions have had any effect on his classroom behavior, which usually ranges somewhere between unsatisfactory to *Get the hell out*. Anthony had done everything from fighting with classmates to stealing from his teachers and sexually harassing his female peers. He'd been expelled from two schools already, kicked out of an alternative program and been locked up in juvenile detention half a dozen times.

Anthony is what most people would refer to as a lost cause. The positive influences at school have had no effect on him, and he had no positive role-model or family member to guide his path at home. There's no guarantee my program will work either, but my success rate with children like him hovers around sixty-percent. Most of the community leaders hear that statistic and applaud my efforts. The mayor has given me a commendation as a matter of fact. But when I hear sixty-percent, I think about the forty percent I couldn't reach.

My program is called *Plan C*. Yeah, I know that's a little lame. But I told you Tremont had a big influence on me. And I know what you're thinking: *How does a pothead loser like me have a program and commendations from the mayor?* Well, that's an interesting story, but I think I can sum it up in a few paragraphs:

When I left Tucker County Jail a decade ago, I had a lot to think about. I thought about race problems. I thought about Tremont, Two Forty Shorty, the guy who got knocked out and the one who got slapped. When I walked out of that building and stepped into the sunlight, I knew I would never get locked up again.

I began to look at the things in my life that led me to jail in the first place. And, you guessed it, marijuana was the number one problem. I had dropped out of school for weed and hadn't done anything productive since my first bong. So when I got back to Ryan's house, I told him I was done smoking weed. That was step one. After that, everything started to fall into place.

Ryan and I had serious personality conflicts when I was sober, so I moved back in with my mom. Happy that I was drug free, she paid for me to go to community college. After a couple of years with only A's and B's, I qualified for a scholarship to Texas Lutheran University. There, I studied counseling and social work. I still remember the look my advisor gave me when I told her what I wanted to do for a living.

"I want to work with poor black kids," I said bluntly.

She advised that for future references, I should probably rephrase that to "*at-risk kids*" or "*disadvantaged youth*," but she was pleased with my aspirations nonetheless.

It took a lot of work, a lot of grants, and a lot of prayers to get Plan C off the ground. My center has been open for four years now. We only have one building so far, but I have a great staff and a great community backing me. We expect to be as big as the Boy's Club one day. Speaking of the Boy's Club, I should point out the differences between my organization and theirs.

First of all, I take in girls as well as boys. We both take kids after school in an attempt to get them involved in positive activities, but that's about where the similarities end. Unlike the Boy's Club, my center is open twenty-four hours a day. We have real-live teachers, and some of the kids we get are court-ordered; meaning they come to me as an alternative to going to jail, and they must remain under my supervision for a specified time period.

Mostly I deal with students on the verge of being kicked out of school. Before the expulsion papers are written up, I get the kids after school every day for three weeks. They have to stay with me from 4:00 pm until bedtime. If after the three-week period they have shown no signs of improvement, the principals are allowed to carry on with their proceedings, but this is where I've had the 60% success rate.

At the center we have fun, games, trips and things of that nature, but education is always our main focus. And our lesson plans range much further than the district's requirements. Tremont was right; if you want to know the real history of black people, you're not going to learn much in school. Students at Plan C learn about Marcus Garvey, Booker T. Washington and Malcolm X. They learn about the Black Panthers and the beauty Langston Hughes saw in his race.

We try to instill a sense of pride and purpose. We're practical with our lessons and nothing is sugar-coated. We tell our kids, "Yes, you may be poor, your mother may be on crack, and you may not have everything laid out at your feet like the white kids across town. But that doesn't mean you can't be whatever you want in this country. The work is going to be harder for you, but the outcome is going to be better than a six by nine cell or a six feet deep hole."

Plan A was messed up, and Plan B was messed up, too. But at my center, we give them the knowledge and understanding to fix *Plan C*.

≈≈≈≈≈≈≈

I find Anthony at the third house I visit. It's his uncle's house. Anthony knows I don't want him at this location. His uncle sells drugs and has admitted to me that he allowed Anthony to smoke pot at his house on several occasions. Anthony sees my car, and the look of guilt he registers is priceless. I pull up to the curb and roll my window down so he can see my face. I have a really stern look I've been perfecting. I flash it on the student in all its glory.

"Anthony. What are you doing here?"

He steps off the porch and walks up to my car. "Nothing, Mr. Harris. Just chilling."

"Where are you supposed to be?"

"At the center," he says dolefully.

"So, why are you here?"

"I dunno. I wanted to kick it with my uncle." He kicks around a few pebbles in the driveway.

"Where's your uncle?" I ask him.

"He not here."

"Who's in the house?"

"His girlfriend."

"What's she doing?"

Anthony looks away, and I know he's going to lie. "Nothing."

"Is she smoking weed?"

He looks the other way. "I dunno."

"Have you been smoking weed?"

"Maybe. Just a little."

I know Anthony is sliding into the lost 40%, but I still have twelve days left before we reach the end of our three weeks together.

"Get in," I tell him.

Anthony's obedient, and I have to take this as a minor success. On the way to the center, I tell him a story about a kid I used to know named Tremont Grant. I tell him about Tucker County Jail, the fights, and the dope house Tremont used to have on Jessamine. Anthony is a good listener, and he's a lot more street-smart than I was at his age. When I tell him Tremont is currently in prison with a football number, Anthony knows exactly what I'm talking about.

SAME GANG

The sun licked the hood of my Chrysler and heated the vehicle like an oven as I bounced along the bad streets on the south side of Overbrook Meadows, Texas. My car didn't have a working AC, and it was already 90 degrees at nine o'clock in the morning. On the radio Tupac crooned about the marvels of living in Los Angeles. The slain rapper did not acknowledge the fact that L.A. County was averaging at least one murder a day, but he did hint that there were undertones of violence beneath the shade of those stunning palm trees.

My little brother sat in the passenger seat neatly folding a bandana as I drove. He gave his flag the same care a Marine might as he removed it from the casket of one of his bullet-riddled comrades. I knew Eddie would defend his lifestyle passionately, but I teased him anyway; mainly because I really wanted him to find a goal in life other than the faux-glory of his colored rags. But I also teased him because it was cool to see him go off sometimes.

"Say, let me see that," I said, reaching for his blue handkerchief. "I'm sweating like a mug over here."

At that moment in life, I had graduated high school with more A's than B's and no C's. I had already enrolled at Texas Lutheran University, a pre-med major at that, but I was not above the vernacular of Ebonics. I didn't even know what *like a mug* meant, but it was as much a part of me as good grades were.

Lil Eddie *never* made a good grade that I knew of, so "*like a mug*" was right up his alley as well. He quickly abandoned folding the flag. He draped it over his lap and then held it up by two corners.

"You wanna wipe your face with this, nigga?"

I grinned and nodded.

"You out your mind, cuz. This here is deep." Lil Eddie dropped the rag and started throwing up the various gang signs of his Crip set as he ranted: "This is *AGG Land*, nigga! 817 G's for life. BK for life, cuz."

Eddie's hands moved so quickly, they almost blurred as he hit me up. My little brother was very fair-skinned, and the tattoos on his forearms stood out against his skin like zebra stripes. One tattoo was "817," printed in large block numbers. On the other arm, "AGG LAND" was scrawled in a column, starting at the top of his forearm and ending at his wrist.

Lil Eddie was only sixteen, but he had already adopted the lifestyle of a hardcore delinquent. He was kicked out of his primary school in Waxahachie for truancy and fighting. He was also kicked out of the alternative school in that city for the same reasons.

Being the son of my stepfather, Eddie Sr., it was decided that Lil Eddie should come live with us in Overbrook Meadows for a while. My mom was a good woman, and she always did whatever she could to help the children Papa Eddie had before he met her. Papa Eddie was the father of seven kids, and they all came to live with us on and off throughout my life. Usually they stayed for five to six months before moving back home to Waxahachie.

I had the *one* family; with my mom, step-father, brother and sister, but I also had another family. All of my step brothers and sisters were pretty rough, but I couldn't fault them individually. Seven kids growing up with one parent in the projects wasn't likely to produce any Rhoades scholars.

Of Papa Eddie's seven offspring, five were boys, and all of them had been locked up at one point or another. Two of my step-brothers were currently in the penitentiary. One of my step-brothers, Damien, had managed to avoid the pen, but he couldn't avoid the city's growing murder rate. The police reported to a *shots fired* call last December and found Damien's body in a motel parking lot.

My mom enrolled Lil Eddie in school when he arrived for his extended visit. He did not make it through the first semester before getting into a gang-related fight. He was now enrolled in his second alternative school, which was our destination that humid morning.

I was older, but because I didn't grow up with him, I never felt like a real big brother to Lil Eddie. I didn't ride him for his bad decisions. In actuality, I found myself getting more involved in his evil deeds rather than the other way around. When Eddie wanted to do a driveby on the guys who jumped him at Poly High School, it was I who drove the getaway car. We did not find our victims on that day, but we did look for them, and we were armed.

I was a good kid, but I was also a hood kid growing up with hoodlums. My high school teachers would have been shocked if they knew about some of the things that when on in my family.

"You do your homework," I asked my step-brother, almost wistfully.

"We ain't have no homework," Eddie said mechanically while digging into one of his front pockets. He produced a small amount of marijuana and clipped a cigar from its perch on his ear. He then began to partake in his 2nd favorite activity. Next to gangbanging, Eddie loved to roll blunts. I would guess the act of rolling a blunt was just as comforting as the smoking of said blunt for him, but I never mentioned it. The pungent odor of weed filled my car as he untwisted the baggie.

Eddie stuck his snout in the bag and took a good whiff. "This shit's the bomb," he announced with a grin.

Knowing Mama would not approve of me allowing Eddie to smoke weed on the way to his Last Chance (Chump) Alternative school, I gave the usual argument:

"Man, you know you ain't supposed to be smoking weed on the way to school."

Eddie smiled as he sliced the cigar open with one of his sharp fingernails. "I ain't gon' get in trouble," he offered. "Yesterday at lunch this teacher tried to get me for smoking weed."

This was news to me. "What happened?"

"She came out there where me and my homies be, and she say she smelled some weed," Eddie explained.

"Why she say that?" I asked.

"Cause I had *just* put it out," he said matter-of-factly. "I don't think she smelled it though." Faulty thinking like that had impaired Eddie for most of his life.

"So what happened?" I asked.

"She took me to the principal's office, but we had to walk all the way around the building, and the wind was blowing kinda hard. By the time we got to him, you couldn't even smell it no more. He say he didn't smell nothing. Told me to go to class – say, where you want me to put this?" He looked around for a receptacle for the cigar's innards.

Before I could suggest the ashtray, Lil Eddie chose his window. The back passenger window was down, however, and a good deal of the tobacco flew back into my car. My Chrysler was a hooptie though, so there was no love loss over a little more debris.

Where you gonna go if you get kicked out of school again? I wanted to know. *Do you have another family in Dallas or Houston that I don't know about? My mama took off half a day of work to get you enrolled in this damned school. Why you wasting everybody's time if you don't wanna do right?*

But I bit my tongue on these questions. None of Papa Eddie's kids had made any drastic improvements at our house, and I wasn't expecting a miracle with Eddie. I'm sure they lived a little better when they came to stay with us, but they weren't here to gobble up three meals a day. They were supposed to be getting *right*, but mostly they just taught me and my brother a little more wrong each time, which is why I took the blunt when Eddie passed it to me.

≈ ≈ ≈ ≈ ≈ ≈

We puffed the cigar like Popeye for a few minutes until we reached the intersection of Allen and Evans. With the windows down, the car didn't fill up with smoke, so I was able to clearly see a crowd of people milling in the street ahead of us. Most of these individuals were hanging out in the parking lot of a convenience store. I quickly recognized one of the ghetto youths as my big brother. My one *real* brother.

James was what one might expect of a street thug. He had an afro that was plaited down to his skull. He wore a black tee-shirt with blue Dickey pants. His white converse had blue shoe strings. Even from a distance, I could see that he was agitated about something.

I was not surprised to see James standing in the middle of a south side street on a Monday morning. Like Lil Eddie, James was an avid gang member. As a matter of fact, James started his very own Crip set not too long ago. His new set gave him a lot of notoriety, mostly from the Overbrook Meadows Gang Unit who had been openly watching him for the past year or so.

James had been to jail more times than I had fingers but had avoided prison thus far. James was large, but not fat. He had a body builder's torso with a thick neck that disappeared into bulging traps, and a barrel chest. At six feet, I stood nearly a full head over my brother, but I was never mistaken for the oldest or the meanest. James was the type of person you would not want to meet in a dark or brightly lit alleyway. But he was my brother, and I loved him as a mother barracuda loves her baby barracudas.

"That's J Cuzz," Lil Eddie announced, referring to James by the name the streets gave him. I never referred to my brother as J Cuzz, and I always felt an underlying pulse of danger when the epithet was uttered.

Eddie stashed his blunt in the ashtray and was out of my car before I came to a complete stop. I watched as he and James greeted each other. I always felt a pang of jealousy when I watched Eddie interact with my brother. *For my own good,* James had shunned me from most of his criminal activities, but he and Eddie were on the same page. They greeted each other with a Crip handshake that I did not know.

James then walked to my car. He approached on the passenger side and stuck his head through the window. His hair was braided back in six uniform corn rolls that glistened in the sun and fell from the back of his head like black mambas. James was handsome and always a ladies' man despite (or possibly because of) his darker than dark complexion that most people would refer to as *blue-black.*

"Get out, cuz. This nigga trying to steal my car!" James barked and turned quickly back to a crowd that was starting to gather.

I didn't see James' Cutlass anywhere, so I wasn't sure how it was being stolen. I pulled to the side of the street and got out despite the NO PARKING sign clearly planted three feet away.

As I rounded the Chrysler towards my brothers, I took in as much of my surroundings as possible. The people standing around were mostly young, black men between the ages of 15 and 25. They watched us with a nonchalance that belied their aggressive tendencies. They were all members of a Crip set called Deuce Land. My brothers were members of the AGG Land Crips.

One might assume all Crips get along, but this is far from the case. In Los Angeles, the origin of the Crip and Blood gangs, most murdered Crips are killed by fellow Crips. This is largely due to the fact that there are far more Crips than Bloods, and people tend to get into it with the folks they see every day.

At that moment there was no bad blood between the Deuce Land Crips and my brother's set, but there was always a degree of uncertainty with any of James' endeavors, especially when he allowed anger to blur his vision.

"What's going on?" I asked when I made it to the man they called J Cuzz.

James could not stand still. He paced with quick, deliberate steps. He scanned the streets in all directions. His fists were clenched. He was livid.

"This motherfucker trying to steal my car!" he said again.

"Who?" I asked as I looked around. There was no sign of his Cutlass anywhere, and the people standing around appeared to be bystanders.

"That nigga *Jojo*," my brother said as if I had some idea who Jojo was. James stopped for a second and gave me his attention. "I'm over here kicking it, right, you know, just kicking it." *Just kicking it* involved some illegal activity nine times out of ten with James. Selling drugs was the most likely scenario. "This nigga come up to me, talking 'bout, *'Say, J Cuzz, let me roll your shit around the corner,'* ya know?"

I nodded.

"So I let him roll it, right?" James went on. "But he keep *fucking* with me! He supposed to been done brought my shit back. He keep rolling by like he gon' stop, and then he'll burn off, laughing, when I walk up to my car! I'ma kick his ass when he get back here!"

I took a deep breath. There it was in a nutshell: This *Jojo* guy asked my brother to drive his car. James allowed him to, but he was disrespecting my brother by not bringing the Cutlass right back. James accused him of *stealing* the car, but it sounded more like a game to me. Jojo had mistaken my brother for one of his playmates.

On a normal day, in some normal place with normal people involved, this might have ended amiably.

Hey, gimme my car, man.

My bad, cuz, I was just playing, and that would be that.

But my brother wasn't normal and the south side of Overbrook Meadows wasn't normal. I knew Jojo would be back with my brother's car soon, but he wasn't going to get the reception he hoped for. James was primed to kick Jojo's ass.

≈≈≈≈≈≈≈

I looked around and saw that the guys loitering around the store numbered about twelve. They watched me and my brothers closely. I wondered if they were more Jojo's friends than James' or vice versa. I didn't recognize many of them, so I expected the worst.

I prayed for more time to cool my brother down. If I could get him to sit in the car with me, I could drive off and talk to him. But the air was suddenly cut by the deep bass line of an Isley Brothers' classic. Ron Isley crooned that he would *always* come back to his lady friend as his brothers harmonized in the background. I was aware of only one vehicle that produced the sound quality I was hearing. This also happened to be the only Cutlass in the hood that rolled around booming the Isley Brothers. My brother's candy coated ride rounded the corner a moment later and something caught in my throat.

I've never been an advocate of violence, especially black-on-black violence, but self-defense had been on my mind since my brothers first started accumulating enemies. I retreated to my Chrysler as most of the crowd made their way towards the Cutlass. James led the pack, teeth clenched and snarling.

I had a .25 automatic stashed in the glove compartment. I had it out and concealed in my front pocket before I fully knew what my intentions were. I turned to see my brother's car coming to a stop ten yards up the street. I could see that the driver was smiling. There was no visible sign of damage to the Cutlass, but James wasn't inspecting his car. His eyes were laced with fire and primed for battle.

Jojo opened the door and stepped gingerly from my brother's ride. His smile was so big I could see that he needed dental work on a few cavities.

"Say, that's a tight–" he began, but the words melted in his mouth when he saw my brother stomping towards him. Jojo managed to get out a quavering, "What's up?" before a speedy right hook connected with the side of his head.

The crowd was immediately electrified. Jojo was spun sideways by the blow. He righted himself and said, "Whatchoo–" before dodging a second punch became more important than talking. He managed to catch most of James' second blow on his shoulder, but it still staggered him. From just those two swings, I knew Jojo was not going to be a factor in the altercation. His fight or flight mechanisms were still searching for a painless compromise. He wasn't exactly running from my brother, but he was backing up quicker than Usain Bolt.

Seeing that J Cuzz was bent on destruction, Jojo hesitantly raised his dukes, but he looked like a child standing up to his father.

The crowd began to circle the men as expected, but I was surprised to hear someone shouting, *"One-on-one! One-on-one!"* which meant no one was to interfere with the fight.

But James connected again with a damaging hook to Jojo's chops, and it was clear that *one-on-one* wasn't going to work for the prankster-turned-car-thief. Jojo looked around frantically for one of his comrades to come to his defense, and they did not disappoint.

I approached the group cautiously and saw that Jojo and James were no longer fighting in the center of the crowd. James was at the core by himself, and balled fists were beginning to rain down on him like hailstones on a tin roof. Out of the corner of my eye, I saw that Lil Eddie was attempting to defend himself from three attackers. Just as I wondered if they'd forgotten me, something slammed into the side of my face, bringing with it a sudden flash of pain and stars that danced before my vision like fairy dust.

I've often heard that in certain times of stress or high emotion, things will move in *"slow motion."* I once doubted this phenomenon, but I can assure you that the next three minutes of my life felt like thirty. The heat wave gave way to an arctic breeze that drifted down my chest and belly. My heart thudded in my chest like George Foreman pounding a heavy bag. Before I was aware of my actions, I heard a voice in the group yell out, "**He got a gun!**"

I looked down to find that I was in fact holding my .25 in plain view.

Within seconds the scene was filled with soldiers scrambling for cover. The "**He got a gun!**" warning was repeated over and over. It echoed down the street, and the gangsters began to retreat from me and my brothers in rapid succession. Few looked back to see who exactly had the gun because details like that don't matter when you're running from the Grim Reaper.

Haltingly, still dizzy from the weed and the blow I'd absorbed, I sought out my brothers. As the large crowd melted away, I saw James emerge from their midst. I didn't think the whole thing had been going on for more than ten seconds, but my brother's condition contradicted this. James looked like he'd taken an orchestrated beating for at least five minutes. I knew this wasn't possible, but I'd never seen blood flow freely from my brother's face. I'd never seen him stagger to a standing position with his tee-shirt ripped almost to shreds, hanging in shards from his frame like Lazarus' dressings.

James screamed something in my direction, but I couldn't understand what he was saying. Adrenaline flooded my system. Blood rushed past my ears with the intensity of a freight train.

My brother was nearly running towards me as he screamed again. It wasn't a sentence. It was one word. It was a dire command, but I didn't understand what he was saying until he was almost upon me.

"Shoot!" he spat. Crimson spittle twinkled in the air. His face contorted with urgency. He was frantic, defeated and demonic.

"Shoot!" he snarled again, and I finally understood the meaning of the word. The meaning was a heavy weight and my knees almost buckled under it. My soul was smothered beneath the implications.

Shoot?

Me?

How could he want that? They were running. They were no longer harming us. They were seeking refuge behind dumpsters, around buildings and under cars. What would my target be? Someone's back? The back of their head? I couldn't believe James would ask that of me. He'd kept me away from his illustrious gang activities by tooth and nail, but now he wanted me to shoot unarmed men as they fled. No college, no med-school, just **BANG-BANG** in someone's spine. James wanted me to be like him. He wanted me to be like Lil Eddie.

Like Damien.

I had only a moment to contemplate this before James was within arm's reach. His face was twisted into a mask of pain, fury, and bitter, bloody vengeance. He ripped the small piece from my limp hand and turned back to his aggressors. There were only five people still in the process of retreat. James fired on them as if the whole Deuce Land set was there.

CRACK!CRACK!CRACK!

The sound of the .25 cut into the commotion like cymbals in an auditorium. Gangsters dove, jumped, ducked and scrambled to safety wherever they could. One of the ghetto boys fell as if hit, but he'd merely tripped over his own feet. He righted himself and commenced a 200 yard dash with Olympic speed.

CRACK!CRACK!CRACK!

The noise was enormous. I'd only test-fired the pistol once, and I didn't remember the gunfire being that loud. It was like firecrackers on the 4th of July.

James continued to squeeze the trigger even after audible clicks indicated the shells were all spent. The block grew eerily quiet then. Not one of the opposing gangsters remained. No one was on the ground injured. No one cried out in pain from their hiding places. The acrid smell of gunpowder wafted around my head.

James spun on me. His voice was high in his throat, and his words were laced with fury. ***"WHY YOU DIDN'T SHOOT?"*** he demanded.

Staring into those deranged eyes, I took a step back. There were plenty of perfectly rational answers to his question bouncing around my skull, but the words got caught in my throat like they were squeezing through a funnel.

"I d–, whuh? James, I–"

"WHY YOU DIDN'T SHOOT?" he screamed again. I noticed that the white of his left eye had a fresh blotch of red in it.

Blood trickled down his cheek from a cut under his other eye. His lip was busted. His nose bloody. He turned away from me angrily before I could put an acceptable response together.

Without looking back, James stomped to his car and got in. I looked at Eddie and saw that he had taken a good deal of punishment also. His bruises appeared worse because they were more pronounced on his light skin. The most significant damage was a shiner centered so perfectly under his right eye, a Hollywood makeup artist would think it was too cliché to reproduce.

I didn't think Eddie would go straight to school, but I was still willing to take him. Instead, he shot me a forlorn look of disappointment and shook his head.

Lil Eddie got into the Cutlass with James. A moment later the car's engine started, and the block was once again filled with the Isley Brothers. They drove away, leaving me standing there amidst two unmatched shoes, broken beer bottles, and a cluster of colored rags that were all the same color.

≈≈≈≈≈≈≈

When I began reading the letter from my brother, I couldn't help but become emotional as I considered that steamy Monday morning four years ago. I never had any serious problems with James after the incident, but we never really talked about it, either. Thinking back, I remember Lil Eddie gave me a hard time longer than James did, but he went back to Waxahachie three months after the incident. James got his first real time, twelve months in state jail, a few weeks after Lil Eddie left. In the past four years, James has been in and out of prison a few more times. He was currently doing sixteen months for a drug charge.

In the years since Jojo decided it might be cool to joy ride in my brother's car, a lot has changed in Overbrook Meadows. The murder rate finally peaked, putting us up there with notoriously bloody cities like Detroit and Chicago. The high crime rate eventually caused the mayor to crack down on gang activity with a vengeance. The plan was to drop the city's annual number of homicides from 300 back down to a respectable 50. They found that putting black and Hispanic delinquents in jail for decades at a time seemed to do the trick.

Last year there were only 72 murders in Overbrook Meadows. The year my brothers and I had the altercation at the intersection of Allen and Evans, there were 322. A lot of people I grew up with are serving life sentences for murder and gang offenses. A lot of mothers miss their sons. Even more kids are growing up without their fathers. As for me, well, I just miss my brother.

I opened his letter expecting a request for money or bikini pictures, but James surprised me by asking if I remembered the time the three of us got jumped. Four years was a long time, but he was crazy to think I may one day forget. What I read next surprised me. It was something that needed to be said, something that might have been said long ago in a different family, but I never thought I'd hear those words from my big brother.

James told me he was sorry for getting mad at me when I didn't fire my weapon that day. He admitted that he was upset with me for a long time, and he thought I didn't shoot because I didn't care about him. But he forgave me now, and he wanted me to forgive him. He said I never should have been put in that position, and he knew that my life might be tragically different if I had pulled the trigger. I wouldn't currently be a senior in college if I took his advice. He said he was proud of me.

I was misty-eyed when I finished reading his letter. Despite all of his faults, James had a way of making you love him. I wrote him back and told him I forgave him a long time ago.

≈ ≈ ≈ ≈ ≈ ≈

I graduated from Texas Lutheran University two months later, not as a medical student, but as a teacher. I believe I can do more in this position to help the youth in my city. Maybe I will have the opportunity to help a kid like me, a kid with little positive guidance and even fewer positive role models in his life, a kid caught in the crossfire of existence who may one day have to make a decision, a quick decision like mine that will affect the rest of his life.

SCENES FROM A MARRIAGE
BY PHYLLIS ALLEN

"Roz, just so you know, marriage is waking up in the morning, realizing he's still breathing, turning over and saying, 'Damn! Another prayer unanswered.' But before the day is over he does something so wonderful that you look at him with love in your eyes and say, 'See, that's why he's my boo.'"

That was Ms. Gladys, my husband's mama, on my wedding day.

She was right.

Edward was a dream come true and yet, I still ended up cleaning the toilet with his toothbrush.

Was I wrong to expect that our marriage would be perfect? Grown children?

We agreed. Edward's son was worthless.

Bills?

We agreed. He believed it was a man's job to pay them and I let him.

Household chores?

We agreed. The cooking and housework, mine. The outside stuff, his.

We agreed. We were happy, until we weren't.

≈ ≈ ≈ ≈ ≈ ≈ ≈

There was no clue on the night that he asked me to be his wife. My car had broken down on the I-20 overpass, causing traffic to back up for miles. Edward drove his wrecker up the side of the freeway, parked the truck on the grassy median and walked

the last quarter mile carrying his tool box. Once he got my car
running and we were going to retrieve his truck, he turned to me
saying, "I worry that if I wasn't in your life, there would be no one
to rescue you."

*Don't get all feminist on me and say that a woman doesn't
need a man to rescue her. I love being rescued.*

He was holding a diamond ring. I said yes.

I'm not the first woman to say yes to a ring. Men know
this. Why do you think they pull out the ring first and then pop
the question? They know that most women are going to say yes to
anything that will result in that rock resting on their finger.

Anyway, what's not to love? The man can fix a car and buy
a perfect two carat, diamond ring.

For three days I walked around with my hand extended
and my wrist bent as if I had been in an awful accident. Anybody
who even glanced in my direction got flashed.

Pow!

The only thing more important than the ring is the
wedding. I had been planning mine since third grade. Back then I
was going to marry Travis Roth, but in spite of a fortune spent on
valentine cards, he managed to grow up to marry my best friend
Sherry. And then there was my first husband. He and I went to
the courthouse and stood in front of a Justice of the Peace. We
were both wrapped in our own personal misery, mine because I
was seven months pregnant and his because he didn't want to get
married.

This time I wanted it done right. I wanted a wedding with
all of my friends and family, a white dress and a cake. There had
to be cake. This wedding was my fantasy.

On the big day, there he stood, looking so damn handsome
in his rented midnight blue tux and silver vest. Walking down that
aisle toward him, all I could think about was how wonderful it
would be, being Mrs. Edward Whitehall.

It was wonderful!

Edward is a gentle man. He was happiest when I was
happy. We didn't argue, much. Everything was perfect, or so I
thought.

On Christmas Eve last year, Edward and I were hosting
Santa Madness, our family gift exchange. Everyone was there.
Edward's brothers and sisters and his mother all showed up at

midnight wearing pajamas. Fried chicken, gingerbread pancakes and Crown Royal-infused eggnog got the party started.

The Santa Claus Slide was interrupted by the doorbell.

Frigid December air rushed by Edward as Rudy, Edward's brother and a tall, barely tan woman stood in the foyer. Edward stared at the woman as if she was bringing a lottery check with his name on it.

"Hey everybody didn't mean to crash your party, but I've been home taking care of Mama, and I ran into Rudy at the store today. He invited me," she said as she removed the cashmere coat that matched her tam and extended it in my husband's direction.

I didn't know it then, but our problems had just walked in trailing a stream of Annick Goutal's Ce Soir Ou Jamais and Glenfiddich scotch.

Want me to puke on your rug? Let me smell either one of those.

"Hi, I'm Roz," I said. "Edward's wife. We're glad you could join us. Rudy, introduce your friend to everybody. Uncle Taylor made the eggnog. It's slamming."

"I already know, pretty much everybody, except for some of the really young ones," our new guest said. "Uncle Taylor you still using real cream in that eggnog?"

"Yeah. Still using a fifth of Crown, too. Just like you like it." Uncle Taylor was grinning at this woman like he'd known her all of his life.

She had incredible green eyes that sparkled with gold flecks. She had a megawatt smile and a way of looking right through you.

Edward stepped out of her line of sight but didn't speak.

Walking through the crushed Christmas wrappings, kid's toys and iPods, the woman made small talk with everyone in the room.

"Angie, I'm glad to see you," she said. "Ms. Gladys, you look good. I'm going to tell Mama that I saw you."

Finally Edward spoke.

"How long have you been in town?" he asked her.

"A couple of months," she said.

"You couldn't call?"

Now I was listening.

"After the last time we talked, I thought it was better that I didn't," the woman replied.

Edward propped himself against the wall and looked down at the floor.

Ms. Gladys, Edward's mama, broke the silence. She spoke to her daughter, "Angie, I know this isn't all my presents. I wanted that Coach bag, and so far it hasn't surfaced. Bring me another gift."

Everybody laughed, and the gift exchange continued. But between *oohing* and *aahing* over their gifts, Angie and everybody else would look at Edward, the woman and then me. When their eyes reached me, they were filled with pity.

Later, all of the gifts had been opened. The kids had begun to fall asleep on their feet. Everybody started packing up their gifts and heading towards home.

At the door, Ms. Gladys told me, "Don't let the past trip up your future baby." She spoke in a whisper.

Before long it was just Rudy, the woman, Edward and I. The woman and Edward sat on the sofa, both leaning forward, speaking in low tones. Rudy was drinking his favorite kind of liquor, free.

As I cleared the leftover party chaos from the living room, I strained to hear what Edward and the woman were saying.

"You know what? This can wait until morning," I decided. "I'm going to bed. Rudy, when you and your friend leave, make sure to lock up," I said, hoping my hint wasn't too subtle.

Nobody answered.

I paused to check the thermostat. Suddenly it was cold.

I went to bed, alone.

After that, Edward became a ghost in our house. If I spoke to him directly, he answered me. But he wouldn't initiate a conversation. Once I watched him dial a number on his phone and hang up at least ten times. Finally he laid the phone on the kitchen cabinet and left the room. Five minutes later he was back, dialing and hanging up again.

A woman, knowing her husband is cheating, waits.

I watched for changes in Edward. If I asked him to move a chair and he didn't do it immediately, I charged it to the fact that he was cheating on me. I couldn't hold my tongue when he didn't take out the trash one day.

"So now I'm supposed to cook your meals, wash your dirty drawers and take out the trash?"

"Huh?"

"Don't huh me. You know you didn't take the trash out this morning."

"I'm sorry," Edward said. "Guess I just forgot. Don't worry about it."

"I don't deal in trash. You do."

That was the first day that I used his toothbrush on the commode.

Edward and I had been so comfortable together. We could sit on the deck, each reading a book or checking our e-mail, our toes barely touching. We would look up at each other and ask, "What's for dinner," at the same time, and we'd smile and laugh.

Now, words eluded us.

Now I sat alone in our dark bedroom, watching the little green dots that etched out time on the clock face. I feigned indifference as it chimed 2 am. Edward's phone had gone straight to voice mail the twenty-two times that I called it, leaving me with ghastly images of him lying dead in a ditch or alive in the arms of the Christmas Eve woman.

At 3 am the phone on the nightstand rang. I stared at it for awhile before I answered.

"Hello."

"Hey Babe." Edward's voice had its usual even tone.

"Where the hell have you been?"

"Stopped off for some drinks with Rudy and a few of his friends."

Frustrated, I hung up on him. I didn't tell him that Rudy had called that morning saying he was headed to New Orleans. Only twenty minutes passed before I heard Edward enter the house. Moments later his silhouette filled the bedroom door, lit from behind by the hall light.

He asked me, "Why'd you hang up?"

I asked him, "Why'd you lie?"

"Lie? About what?"

Turning over, I pulled the covers over my head. I didn't want to look at him, standing there with his white shirt open at the collar, stinking of another woman and looking so damn good all I wanted was to beg him not to leave me.

He flipped off the hallway light and sat on the side of the bed.

"You might want to shower first," I told him.

"What are you trying to say?"

"Thought I said it. You might want to shower first."

"What I really want is to talk to you," Edward said. "Without the sarcasm."

"Not tonight."

Please God not tonight, is what I was thinking.

"We need to talk."

"Not tonight. Wait until morning. Just go to bed. We'll talk in the morning."

As soon as he was snoring, I slid out of bed, got dressed and left the house. I drove aimlessly.

Hours later, sitting in front of Pamela's house (yep that's the Christmas Eve woman's name, Pamela Anne Dameron), I called my friend Marsha on my cellphone.

"What do you hope to prove?" she asked me.

"I want to see her."

"And then what?"

"I don't know. I want her to tell me what I already know. And then I want to make Edward choose, me or her."

"Are you ready for that?"

For the second time in twenty-four hours, I hung up on someone. I didn't know what I wanted anymore.

≈ ≈ ≈ ≈ ≈ ≈

Back at home, Edward's mind was in similar disarray:

Turning over and finding my wife gone, I just realized how serious this situation is. Sleeping around behind her back is destroying our marriage. I feel just like my old man, a liar and a cheat.

Marrying Roz was the happiest day of my life. Standing there at the altar and watching her walk down the aisle toward me, I felt so proud that this beautiful woman chose me.

We are so much alike, and the ways that we aren't adds spice to our relationship.

Everything that I wanted for so long, I now have; a beautiful wife, a new house. Roz's son Damon is the son that I

143

never had. Not that I don't have a son, I do, but he's almost forty and still living at home with his mom.

Roz and I were happy.

And then Pamela came back.

Every man has a Pamela Anne Dameron in his life. She is a woman whom he has loved for as long as he has known her. She is bad for him, but he will drink her bath water just to get a taste of her.

That's my Pamela.

I met her in high school. We were walking home, and she decided that I should carry her books. Most people would ask you nicely, not Pamela. She'd cross those long legs, and you'd lift her house if she asked you to.

First it was carrying her books, and then it was taking my last two dollars to buy her cigarettes or a beer from the bootleg man.

Pamela was fifteen, going on middle age.

At her house, when her mama wasn't home, she could wrap her long legs around my back and I saw heaven. Really, I saw God's face, angels, everything.

She was sixteen when she told me that she was pregnant.

It was three days past my eighteenth birthday. Uncle Sam had sent me an impersonal invitation to a family party. Problem was, it wasn't my family, and it was a helluva long way from home.

Pam and I got married. I went off to boot camp, and she moved in with my mom. My number came up right out of boot camp, and off I went to the party. After the sweat, mosquitoes and misery of Vietnam, coming home to a young wife seemed like paradise.

Paradise quickly morphed into hell.

My mom hadn't told me in the letters she wrote that Pamela spent most nights out, leaving her to walk the floor with a crying baby. Nothing changed when I came home, except that instead of my mom it was me walking the floor.

Pamela wanted everything that life had to offer, and very quickly she found someone else to give it to her.

She left me.

We didn't argue over the baby. Pamela left him, too.

At the divorce hearing, Pamela and her new man wore matching lime green outfits and huge afros. Pamela's attorney assured the judge that all his client wanted was her freedom. The judge gave it to her, and off Pam went, out of the courtroom and my life.

Three months later, her sugar daddy collapsed on her during an *intimate moment*. Two days after that, Pamela and her lime green suit wearing self showed up on my doorstep.

In spite of everything, my first thought was, "Damn she looks good."

Ignoring my mom's warnings, I let Pamela move back in. We were happy. It was the honeymoon we never had. Pam played at being a wife and mom.

And then she was gone again. Six months later she called from Los Angeles, no apology, just wanted money to come home. I sent it. The plane arrived, but she didn't.

For the next ten years, Pamela came and went, marching through my life like the Viet Cong through the Mekong Delta, leaving a wake of destruction behind her.

A drained bank account, impounded vehicle and broken nose are just a few of the low points, but the highs were intoxicating. Pamela knew how to get into my head. My heart was as open to her as her legs were to me.

I woke one morning, looked over at Pamela and realized love wasn't enough. We had to stop.

My son and I moved out that day.

Starting over was hard, but without the distraction of Pamela's erratic behavior, it was doable. There were no midnight phone calls, no strange men knocking on the door in the middle of the night, and no surprises when bills were due. I had peace. But there were no long legs wrapped around my middle, either. There were no bottle green eyes pleading with me for forgiveness, no high-highs, but no crashing lows.

Life in my house had revolved around Pamela for so long, I lost touch with my teenage son, leaving him vulnerable to the seductive wiles of his mother. Unable to sway me, Pamela turned her attention on our son. And when the smoke cleared, he was living with her. He still does, almost twenty years later.

After Pamela, I swore off women.

And then I met Roz.

My best friend Charles and his wife Jay were convinced that Roz and I were perfect for each other. I resisted the many times they tried to hook us up. I made excuses. Can't come to dinner tonight, I've got bible study. Barbecue on Saturday? Sorry, can't.

One day I opened the door, and Roz was standing on my porch.

"Look you don't have to invite me in," she said. "But Charles and Jay sent me over to invite you to dinner. In two weeks, at their twenty-fifth anniversary party, they're renewing their vows. I'm the matron of honor, and you're the best man. They thought we should meet."

"Okay."

We stood looking at each other, both of us confused as to what our next move should be.

"Well, I guess I'll see you when we go down the aisle," Roz said.

She turned to walk away, and I noticed she had a great ass.

"Wait. Would you like to come in?"

When she turned back around, it was Roz's beautiful smile that captured my heart.

Wine lubricated our conversation. We talked for hours, though it seemed like only minutes. Every question was about me. Instead of feeling high around Roz, I felt leveled. The time we spent together passed too quickly.

Roz brought order to the chaos that was my life. Asking her to marry me just seemed natural. When she said yes, I was happy for the first time in years.

And then on Christmas Eve, the door opened and Pamela was back. Damn her! We are no good together. But I can't help thinking that maybe, at this time in our lives, it will be different.

I don't want to hurt Roz, but...

≈ ≈ ≈ ≈ ≈ ≈ ≈

Maybe counseling was the answer. Edward would've suggested it, but he already knew what everyone would say. As a matter of fact, he could've written a script:

Roz: "I still love Edward with all my heart. I gave up believing that someone like Edward would appear in my life. Ours is an age old story with each familiar part represented. I love Edward so much that my heart hurts. Edward loves me, but..."

Edward: "Yeah, I love Roz. She's terrific, but..."

Pamela: "Edward has always taken care of me. I know that no matter what, he loves me. We've been together for over forty years. He's always loved me. What if no one else ever loves me like him?"

Roz: "All I want is the husband that I married. We have, we *had* a good life, before she showed up. I believe that we can again, if she goes away."

Edward: "Pamela is so different this time. She cooks for me. She's got a job and a house that she bought with her own money. When I'm with her, it seems like we're right back in 1972 and getting everything right. We didn't make it work before. I'm sure we can this time, but..."

Pamela: "We don't deserve to spend the rest of our lives wondering if we could have made it work this time. After all, it says in the bible that what God has joined together, let no one separate."

Roz: "Amazingly, Edward still says that he loves me. But what does that mean? If this was a movie, it would be easy; Pamela, a bad woman, would lose. But this isn't the movies. This is real life."

Edward: "Roz, the last thing I want to do is hurt you. I do love you, a lot. But Pamela and I have too much history to ignore. Whatever you want is yours. I don't want you to suffer because of this."

Roz: "You'll pardon me if I don't wish you good luck. I never wanted you to leave."

Edward: "Yes she did. It was Roz's decision. She sat in front of Pamela's house one night waiting for me to come out. Got right in my face screaming, '*Choose! Dammit you choose right now! It's me or her.*' Maybe if I had more time to sort out my feelings... But when she put it like that, I had no choice. I couldn't lose Pamela. Not again. I still love Roz, but..."

≈≈≈≈≈≈≈

"Child, I can't believe that my son, the one I raised, has ruined his life, again." Miss Gladys spoke aloud as she pondered her son's dilemma.

Men are all the same. Doesn't matter if it's your daddy, husband or son, they all got a weakness for long legs that open at the drop of a zipper.

The first time he brought Pamela to my house, in that little bitty skirt that showed more of her ass than it covered, she was ordering him around like she owned him.

"Get me a glass of water. Edward, I want to go."

Every time she said something, *anything*, he's off like a flash, doing whatever she asked. When I told him that girl was trouble, did he listen? Hell no. Forty years later she's still ruining his life.

And Roz, bless her heart, she wasn't smart. I tried to warn her not to let the past ruin her future, because I knew. Pamela is an aging beauty, and it's clear she's looking for reassurance. Women like her get scared at the first sight of a wrinkle.

The night she walked into Edward and Roz's house, she flexed her emotional muscle over him, made him want her so bad he couldn't think straight. She sat there looking me straight in the eyes, talking about Jesus and how she was living her life for the Lord. Hmph. Someone living for the Lord doesn't lean over and flash a married man with her brand new five thousand dollar titties.

Has she never heard that '*Thou shalt not steal*'?

And now what?

Pamela lured Edward away from his happy home. It could last a month or even a year, but eventually she will need reassurance from someone else. Pamela's damn near sixty, but whores don't change.

They get religion, wear longer dresses and quote bible scriptures, but they're still a whore. Pamela never put anyone's happiness ahead of her own, not my son's or her son's.

When Pamela dumps him, it will be me who picks up the pieces and nurses Edward through his broken heart. But I'm not as young as I used to be.

Edward keeps telling me, "Maybe it won't be like the last time."

When will he learn that it's always like the last time?

≈ ≈ ≈ ≈ ≈ ≈ ≈

"We are happy", Edward repeated to himself, trying to make it a reality.

Everything is different now. Pamela was wild before, always laughing, unpredictable and full of surprises. So what if some of them were unpleasant?

Now the Lord sleeps in our bed. He governs our every decision. The other day I wanted to have another piece of chocolate pie, but evidently He frowns on seconds.

I've joined Pamela's mega church. Sunday mornings are spent attempting to get there early enough to get a parking space close to the building. Hasn't happened yet, not even the morning we got there at seven am.

Flannel pajamas have replaced the warmth of brown skin tucked into fresh linen. The Lord doesn't like nakedness, naughty words or any sex.

Pamela spends a lot of time at church. There is so much for which to repent.

Our son, Brendan, who doesn't work and sleeps until noon, lives with us. Pamela won't hear of his moving. Says that she wasn't there for him when he was young, and now she has a chance to be a mother.

A mother?

He's a thirty six year old man, way past the mothering stage.

"There is a bond between a mother and a son," Pamela told me. "A special one. When the time is right, Brendan will leave and find his own way. Right now he needs me, and he needs you."

"What the hell does he need me for?" I asked her. "I was there. I sacrificed and raised him. My job is done."

"He never had a family."

"Whose fault is that?"

"It's our fault," Pamela said.

I told her, "You can't rewrite history. The truth is that you couldn't be bothered. You walked out on me. You walked out on him, too. It's a sad story, but that's the past. He has to get over it and get on with his life."

"He is getting on with his life."

"No. He's not. He's lying here letting you take care of him. You are stealing his manhood."

"How dare you accuse my son of not being a man."

"He's my son, too. Remember?"

Brendan was at the center of many of our daily fights. Pamela's regrets and mine met at Brendan's bedroom door.

More and more I found myself hiding out in the garage, staying late at work. And then one Wednesday evening I stopped at Mama's to pick up my mail

Opening the door, I found a surprise. Roz was there.

≈≈≈≈≈≈≈

"Hi," Edward said.

"What? Oh, yeah hi."

Roz was perched on the edge of Mama's sofa, studying the pattern of the carpet as if there was going to be a test later. Flipping through the stack of mail addressed to me, I pretended not to be affected by her presence.

Mama was pulling freshly baked sweets from the oven and at the same time keeping a running dialogue with Roz, "So are you going?"

"No, Ma'am. I don't think it's a good idea."

"How do you expect to move on if you don't get out?"

Roz didn't answer. Instead she looked and spoke to me.

"I had to replace the kitchen floor," she said.

"Yeah, we had been saying that for a while," I replied. "Who'd you get?"

"Called someone out of the Yellow Pages."

"Did he do a good job?"

"She did an excellent job."

"What kind of wood?"

"It's teak. She used stainless steel as an edging. It's really cool."

Leaning back on the sofa, Roz relaxed. Mama came in holding two slices of peach pie. Sitting one in front of each of us, she stood looking like the mama who used to serve me and my buddies brownies after school.

"Either one of you want some ice cream on that?"

Simultaneously we answered, "Me. I do."

Our laughter erased any lingering discomfort. We started to talk.

Mama's phone rang at nine. She answered it in the kitchen. She stuck her head around the corner, "Edward, it's for you."

I went to answer it.

Roz stood, brushing pie crust crumbs from her lap.

"I really should be going. Miss Gladys the pie was off the chain, like always."

"Baby, I packed you some leftovers so you can have lunch for tomorrow," Miss Gladys said.

"Thank you," Roz replied. "Is there peach pie in there?"

"Two pieces and some fried chicken, too."

"Thank you so much. I didn't intend to stay so long."

"Pamela's in there giving him grief," Gladys confided, "because Edward didn't go to bible study. Bible study, really?"

By the time I got back to the living room, Roz was backing her car out of the driveway. I stood in the front door and watched Roz drive away. I wanted to go with her.

"You're in deep son," my mother said. "But it's not too late to dig yourself out."

I hadn't even heard Mama walk up behind me. She put her soft hand on the side of my face, and I noticed for the first time that Mama's hands were twisting in the grips of arthritis. Memories of being five years old flooded back. I remembered how Mama's hands could hold back any problem facing me.

"Lord knows a man can do foolish things sometimes," she said. "But that doesn't make him a fool."

"Sometimes a man waits too long to fix his foolishness." I sighed. "I'd better go home. Pamela is already mad about me missing church. No point in making it worse."

"Baby, this is Mama. Are you happy?"

"I'm not sure that I even know what happiness is."

"Roz isn't happy. That woman loves you. It's good to be with someone who loves you."

"You think I screwed this up, don't you?"

"I'm an old woman. It doesn't matter what I think."

"I've made my choice," I told her. "Now I've got to go home and live with it."

"Your son needs to get up and get himself a job,"

"Well that's something to include in your prayers tonight, 'cause the Lord is the only one that can make that happen."

"You could."

"I'm going to talk to him. Pamela wants me to wait until after he gets back from vacation."

"Vacation? What the hell is he vacationing from?"

"It's hard work sleeping 'til noon and scratching your butt."

We both laugh.

Leaning against the door after she closed it, Gladys whispered a prayer.

"Lord, help that boy. A man, in spite of his strength, is weak. He needs You to guide him out of this mess he created."

≈≈≈≈≈≈

The garage door had barely lowered when Roz's cell phone rang. She stood staring at the digitally lit numbers, until the ringing stopped.

It started again almost immediately.

The phone extended from her body, like a snake that might bite. The number flashed. Leaning against the wall for support, she answered.

"Hello."

"How come you didn't answer?" Edward asked. "I just wanted to make sure you got home okay."

Roz pressed the END button, folded the phone and retrieved her bags from the car.

Five minutes later the doorbell rang.

Edward pressed the bell once and then continuously, until the door opened slightly.

"What do you want?" Roz was less than inviting.

"To talk, for just a minute. There are things that I need to explain to you. You've got to believe that I never meant to hurt you. Never."

"The other day I was reaching into the cabinet to get a bowl on the top shelf," she said. "My grandmother's turkey platter slid out, hit the floor, broke into a million pieces. I didn't mean to break it, but it's gone just the same."

"I always hated that damn platter," Edward replied. "Looked like that turkey was staring right at me. I couldn't eat dinner."

It was quiet, and then Roz laughed until she was holding her sides. Edward laughed as well, and he took that moment to slip into the foyer. Roz continued to laugh until he touched her shoulders. Like a faucet, the laughter cut off and the quiet returned, reverberating off the walls.

"You need to leave. Now."

"I know, but I need to talk to you. Tonight, at Mama's, I realized how much I missed talking to you. There are two things that we could always do, talk and–"

"Don't! Don't you dare come in here and try to make everything all better by being cute and saying the things that you know I want to hear. We could talk and we could fuck. That still didn't make you love me."

"I did love, I mean, I do love you. Never stopped. What Pamela and I have goes beyond that. It's like we been con–"

"You need to leave."

"Roz, please. Listen, please."

"When I wanted you to talk, you didn't, wouldn't. You wanted to go be with the love of your life. Did you ever teach your son to be a man? Remember when you told her that?"

"You heard that?"

"That and a lot more. Late at night when I can't sleep, I replay those tapes."

"Tapes?"

"Yep, that's how desperate I was. I taped your phone conversations and I listen to them over and over, trying to find out what I did wrong. But no matter how many words I hear, there is never a clue. She talked about her, and so do you, but nothing in there is about me or you."

Edward pressed his back against the wall and lowered his head. The new wood floors gleamed.

"I like the floors."

"Fuck the floors! You tell me why! That's all that I want to hear from you. Why?"

Edward straightened himself and walked out of her home yet again.

≈≈≈≈≈≈≈

"You didn't talk to him?" Miss Gladys asked.

153

"Of course not," Roz told her.

"What do you mean, of course not? He's your husband. Yours, not hers. And that means something. A man and his wife should be able to talk about anything. Don't forget, when you marry, the preacher says, '*For better or worse.*' And right now, this is the worst."

"Miss Gladys, you don't understand."

"Don't understand? You think Edward invented being an ass? He didn't. His daddy was an ass years before Edward. But he loves you."

Roz shook her head. "No. Not now. He hurt me."

"Boo-hoo. You been hurt. Well join the club. Our numbers are huge. People get hurt."

"What would people say if I forgave him?"

"Who gives a damn? People always got their lips stuck into someone else's business."

"When I wanted to talk to him, he didn't want to talk."

"I never said he wasn't stupid."

Roz smiled. Miss Gladys invented telling it like it is.

"He says he's in love."

"That don't mean shit. He's been saying that since high school. Guess what? Lust and love are both four letter words. You want your husband back?"

"I didn't want him to leave."

"Tell him that. The judge hasn't ruled on your divorce, so there's still time. You two are joined in God's eyes and in the eyes of the law."

"Miss Gladys, you don't know how bad it hurt watching Edward pack his stuff and go. I don't want to hurt again."

"Baby, believe me, I know. But sometimes you got to sacrifice to be happy."

Roz stared at her feet. Edward told her that he loved Pamela, always had. She couldn't risk hearing that again.

"I'll think about it. But no matter what I decide, I'm a real lucky woman."

"Why are you lucky?"

"Because you love me."

Miss Gladys confirmed that with a warm smile.

A few minutes later, Roz had to leave. Miss Gladys saw her out and then watched as Roz backed into the street.

Closing the door, Miss Gladys clutched her left side. The pain there caused her to gasp. Shakily, she sat in the nearest chair. She closed her eyes and leaned back, waiting for the pain to subside.

The beans she was making for Edward's dinner cooked to perfection, scorched and then burned. Gladys couldn't smell them. After that day, Edward never ate beans again.

≈≈≈≈≈≈≈

Roz's phone rang. It was Edward. She started not to answer, but remembering her conversation with Miss Gladys, she relented.

"Hello."

"Are you home?"

"Yeah, I just came in. What's up?"

"I'm at Mama's, and, and something happened over here. My mama, she gone, Roz. Mama gone."

Edward's voice was far away. Roz slid down the wall. Her screams filled the void created by the words.

Two hours later Edward found her huddled in the closet, dry-eyed and heaving. Roz wrapped herself around his legs, almost causing Edward to lose his balance.

Roz spoke in ragged croaks instead of words, "I was just there. She made me dinner."

"I came by after work. She was sitting in her chair. I thought she was sleep."

Edward sank down next to Roz. They held each other and rocked slowly.

≈≈≈≈≈≈≈

In spite of Edward being one of six children, he and his mother were bound tightly. The first day after her death, Edward found himself pulling into Miss Gladys' driveway, but he didn't remember making the drive. Opening the door, he fully expected her to call out, 'In the kitchen, Baby.'

Instead his sister Lizzy was debating whether their mother's last fashion statement should be pink linen or gray silk.

Unable to enter the house full of his mama's essence but empty of her, Edward returned to his truck and sat in the driveway.

Roz found him there.

"Hi."

"Hey."

"Who's in the house?"

"Lizzy and Charles are in there," Edward said. "She's picking out something for Ma—" His voice broke, and his head fell forward.

Leaning in through the open driver's window, Roz cradled Edward's head and rocked slightly.

"It's going to be okay. I promise."

"How? How is it going to be okay? Mama was my best friend. There was never anything that I couldn't tell her."

"I know. Come on, get out."

"Not now," Edward said. "If I go in there, Lizzy will want to ask me about Mama's dress, her hair, whether her glasses should be on or off. I can't do that. No matter where I look, I can't find my mama."

Roz opened the door. "Here, move over. Let me drive us somewhere."

Edward relaxed, slid across the bench seat, leaning his head against the window. Roz got in and cranked the truck. Backing carefully out of the driveway, she eased into the flow of residential traffic and drove aimlessly for fifteen or twenty minutes. Without planning to, she eventually pointed the truck in the direction of her house. It wasn't until the garage door started to go down that Edward looked at her.

"I just thought that you needed to be somewhere that no one could find you for a little while," Roz said.

Edward laid his head in her lap. The sobs shook both of them.

"Come on," Roz said. "Let's go inside."

They supported each other until safely inside. Roz went to the fridge and retrieved a beer. Popping the top, she slid it across the counter to Edward.

"You're still buying Shiner beer?"

"Nope. That's what you bought before you left."

He winced, turned up the bottle and drained it.

"Got another one?"

Still in the fridge, she handed another bottle over her back. She then retrieved foil wrapped packages from the freezer.

"You need to eat. Won't take but a minute, and I'll have something ready."

"That's what Mama would say," Edward replied. "She believed that good food could cure anything, from a broken heart to a broken neck."

"Matter of fact, this is Miss Gladys' meatloaf, mac and cheese and the chocolate cake she sent home with me the other day. She made me food packages about once a week. I'd get a call, *'Baby, stop by here on your way home. I made you some gumbo.'* Once she cooked me an entire dinner. She was an incredible woman."

Draining his second beer, Edward nodded.

Opening the oven with one hand and the fridge with the other, Roz placed the food in the oven while grabbing another beer, which she placed in front of Edward.

"Thanks. I really need the beer – and the company, too."

Roz didn't respond. The oven timer ticked off the silence.

Edward's thick finger traced a line from Roz's shoulder to her hand. He raised her fingers to his lips. Leaning forward, Edward pulled Roz to him.

"Come here."

She folded into his arms. Closing her eyes, her lips parted. His lips and hers together was familiar, like coming home. Edwards hand on her breast caused Roz's breath to come in moist pants. His tongue moved down her throat, her chest, across the thin silk of her blouse, making her anxious for his fingers to release each button and resume his hot, wet journey.

Together they stood in a synchronized dance, slowly making their way to the sofa, leaving a tangled trail of discarded clothing, like crumbs to find their way back. Edward's tongue traced the warmth of her belly button. When he reached his mark, Roz arched toward him, cradling the back of his head and allowing herself to be washed away by the wetness of Edward's tongue and her emotions.

The insistent, pulsing beat of the oven timer provided the soundtrack to their mutual release.

≈≈≈≈≈≈≈

Expensive black silk suit, pearl rope and earrings, hands sheathed in black lace and a hat with a veil transformed Pamela into Hollywood's image of grieving. Her nose wrinkled in distaste.

"Well thankfully this is all over. I had to miss bible study. It's just a shame."

Edward, sitting at the kitchen table, pleated and smoothed the flowered paper on which his mama's obituary was printed. Obituary? It just didn't seem possible that Mama was gone.

"Edward, I'm ready to go," Pamela told him.

Across the room, Roz glanced over her shoulder at Edward. Roz's arms were filled with dirty plates and debris from the repast.

"I said I'm ready to go, Edward," Pamela repeated. "Tonight is my circle meeting, and I've missed enough church as it is. Let's go."

Edward raised his head and looked at her. He was having trouble focusing or processing her words. His brother Rudy responded for him.

"Pamela, I'll make sure that he gets home."

Removing her veiled hat, Pamela looked unsure. She looked across the room at Roz. The apron, house shoes and hair net satisfied Pamela that it was safe for her to leave.

"Edward, when will you be home?"

Without looking at her, he said, "Later."

"Now look, I'm just trying to–"

Rudy held up his hand. "I'll get him home at a decent hour. We've got some stuff to talk about here. Then I'll bring him home."

"Well fine. I won't be there."

Stopping to retrieve Brendan from the den, Pamela left.

Edward lowered his head to the table top, and within seconds his shoulders started to shudder.

Roz continued to clear the kitchen, and she began to sing softly. When a Black woman goes to the Lord, everybody takes notice.

"Lord, this old world is not my home
I'm tired Lord, and I feel so all alone"

People started to come out from other rooms. They stopped and peeked into the kitchen to see who was singing. Unaware of her growing audience, Roz began to sing louder.

"I place my hand in your hand
Lord, on a distant shore I will stand
And wait for You
To lead me on"

Raw emotions, barely hidden beneath the thin veneer of social grace, rose to the surface. Tears started to flow, mingling with reminiscences of Ms. Gladys.

Elizabeth said, "Ooh that was Mama's favorite song. I would come in here, and she'd be making a pie or frying some fish and singing that song."

Rudy followed, "Yeah Mama loved them gospel songs. But she could sing some blues, too. I used to like to hear her sing, *Goin' Down Slow*. She'd sit here late at night. I'd get out a bottle of gin, and she'd get the pork skins. We'd sit at that table, play bid whist and listen to Bobby Bland or B. B. King, and she'd sing along."

They came forward with stories of enjoying music with Miss Gladys. When every story had been told, Edward raised his head from the table.

"Me and Mama used to sit at the table and talk. She was the only person–" Instead of finishing his sentence, Edward's woeful scream filled the air.

The room fell silent.

Taking his arm, Roz led him down the hallway to his mama's room.

≈ ≈ ≈ ≈ ≈ ≈

Back at home, Edward and Pamela's relationship was nearing its inevitable conclusion. They argued more than talked to each other nowadays.

"You're sick," Pamela told him, "jealous of your own son. He's my baby, and I am going to take care of him."

"Baby? He's damn near forty years old," Edward countered. "When are you going to let him grow up?"

"He's grown right now."

"Grown men don't sleep in a twin bed in their mama's house."

"This is his house, too."

"Is it my house Pamela? Is it my house as well?"

"Ever since your mama died, you've been impossible," she snapped. "Is this your house, Edward? That's up to you. Maybe you want to move back over there with your precious *Roz*. You'd like that wouldn't you? Those old woman shoes and her head tied up like Aunt Jemima, that's what you want."

"What I don't want is to work and pay the room and board for a full grown man."

"Then maybe you don't want to be here."

"Maybe I don't."

"If you choose to leave, you can't come back."

Edward gave her words the gravity they deserved before he left. He drove around a while and then headed to Roz's house. He found her in the front yard trimming the shrubs. She turned, stood and walked over to his truck.

"What's up?"

"Nothing. I was just out riding, and thought I would drop by and see what you're up to."

"Well you can see what I'm up to. Want a beer?"

"Yeah, that would be nice."

He got out of the truck. When he was living at home, Roz never even came out in the yard. Now she had transplanted shrubs, dug a new flower bed and learned to use the lawnmower.

"You're becoming quite the gardener," he commented.

"No choice."

They sat on the steps, him drinking a beer and her draining a bottle of spring water, each lost in their own thoughts.

"More and more you remind me of Mama."

"Never a good thing for a woman to remind a man of his mama."

"There are always exceptions."

"I miss her."

"At least once a day I pick up the phone to call her."

He reached for her.

"Don't start this."

"I think I made a mistake."

"You did, but it's done now."

"Not really. The divorce isn't final. We could reconsider."

"No. We're not going to reconsider. It's done, all except for the paperwork. Stop bouncing between Pamela and me like some demented tennis ball. It's over."

Roz stood. She scooped up the two empty bottles, entered the house and locked the door behind her. After five or ten minutes, she heard Edward's truck back out of the driveway.

≈ ≈ ≈ ≈ ≈ ≈

Mama's house, devoid of her possessions, was cold, empty and Edward's only sanctuary. Returning to Pamela's after their last argument was not an option. Roz wasn't accepting his calls. Edward was alone for the first time in his life.

Unable to sleep in Mama's room, he set up his newly purchased bed in what had been known as "the boys" room when he was growing up. The new sheets, pillow and bedding made the room look more like home than he thought possible.

Nights spent crouched in front of his tiny thirteen inch television transported him away from the uncertainty of his future. Content was unimportant. He watched a show on making crepes with the same intensity as the seventh game in a NBA playoff series. His phone rang so infrequently, that when it did it startled him.

Another silent evening loomed ahead of Edward when the doorbell rang. Opening the door, he was surprised to find Brendan standing there with a suitcase in hand.

Brendan started in, looking down tentatively at his suitcase.

"Come in," Edward said with a nod.

Inside the house, Brendan sat his suitcase down and stood looking at his father.

"What's going on?"

"Mom says she wants me out."

"Her *baby*?" Edward asked sarcastically.

An expression, a cross between a smile and grimace, telegraphed Brendan's discomfort.

"She wanted me to get a job. Now that she's going to get married to the preacher, she wants me out."

"Getting married?"

"Yeah, she's marrying that preacher from her church. He used to come to the house calling her Sister Whitehall and acting all holy. Then one morning I busted him trying to slip out of her bedroom."

Edward felt a knot in the pit of his stomach at the news that Pamela was getting married. But it wasn't the devastating blow he would have expected. Felt more like a door being closed and locked.

"You're welcome to stay here, but I'm not your mama. A job? You've got exactly one month to get one. Pay rent? You will pay rent and save money to get your own place. You are a grown man, and I won't do your laundry, make your dinner or clean up behind you."

Brendan looked back at the door, evaluating his options, before he said, "Okay."

Edward led Brendan down the hall to his new quarters. A bed, chest of drawers and a ladder back chair were the only furniture in the room.

"Sheets are in the hall closet, and check out time is one month from today."

"Dad, I'm sorry."

"About what?"

"Everything."

"Basketball game is on. Want a beer?"

His son smiled. "Say man, when you getting a real TV?"

≈≈≈≈≈≈≈

"Brendan looks really good. Living with you agreed with him."

"Yeah, but him moving out, agreed with me."

Roz and Edward were sitting in his newly remodeled kitchen.

"The house is really coming along. Miss Gladys would have cooked herself into a tizzy in this kitchen."

"That's the one thing I regret; Mama isn't here to enjoy all of this. Brendan was a big help. He totally remodeled his bedroom."

"Everything seems to be working out for you," Roz noticed.

"Most things."

She smiled.

"Well, just keep working. Everything will fall into place."

"You're right," Edward said. "You're being an ass, but you're right. Pamela was over here the other day. She and the Reverend just got back from Jamaica. Seeing her didn't affect me at all. When she came in, I spoke and went to my bedroom."

"Bet you were hoping she'd follow you and fill you with some of that Holy Spirit she's got."

"Nope, I wasn't," Edward said. "For the first time since I met Pamela, I didn't want to sleep with her."

"Hmm."

"Now you, that's a different matter. Want to go to my bedroom?"

An awkward silence descended around them. Roz looked up at Edward and smiled.

"Not today. Not tomorrow. But who knows? Play your cards right and soon, very soon, I just might."

COLORED RAGS

CHAPTER ONE
KICK HIS ASS!

"See. *Looka here.* It's shit like this piss me off."

William Broadnax sat up in his Cutlass Supreme and surveyed the block. His younger brother Andre sat in the passenger seat gnawing on a greasy burrito. Will's shiny .45 rested on the seat between them. Hearing Will's displeasure, the pistol wanted a taste. But this predicament required no firearms.

Will and his brother sat in the parking lot of Rainbow Gas and Grocery. The convenience store was not the safest place to get hot foods, but Dre was a fat kid, so that didn't matter. Rainbow was a great place to loiter and sell dope, and Will's black on black Cutlass, sitting on twenty-inch rims, was like a magnet for dopefiends. Will had conducted four transactions in the past thirty minutes but still found something to get upset about. Will never went too long without wrinkling up his nose about something.

"You know who that is, don't you?"

Dre looked up at the individual in question but didn't see anything out of the ordinary. It was Sydney. Sydney was fair-skinned, grimy in his attire, and was addicted to crack cocaine. He walked by with the same worried, hesitant look he always had. There was nothing in his hands. That was *kind of* odd, because Sydney usually had something to barter with rather than actual cash.

"That's Sydney. What about him?"

"That's Sydney," Will agreed. "Where he going?"

Dre hated these pop quizzes. How the hell was he supposed to know where Sydney was going? Will had them backed into the parking spot, so Dre had a good view of the neighborhood, but nothing looked different than the day before. Sydney was on the sidewalk ahead of them headed east, towards Riverside Dr. Dre had no idea what his brother wanted to hear.

"I don't know," he said. "He gon' score from somebody else?"

"Yeah," Will said. "And why he gon' do that?"

Dre felt the temperature rising. "He owe you some money?"

Will nodded, his eyes on the offender. "You see he ain't looked over here, ain't you?"

Dre did notice the crackhead was avoiding eye contact. Sydney was usually very observant, scanning the ground for anything that might be money or might be worth money. Today he kept his face forward, his eyes glued to a destination ahead of him. Dre turned and watched his brother.

Will didn't close his mouth when not speaking, so his bottom lip hung downwards. A little spittle glistened on it. He was still handsome, though, with a strong jaw-line, dark skin, and menacing eyes. Just six months back on the streets after a two year bid, Will was cut like an action figure; big chest, big arms, big shoulders and no gut. Hoochies fought over who got to braid his hair.

At thirty-two, Will was considered *old school*. He led a rough group of Crips who had developed a stronghold on the city's south side. Dre thought Will should be happy about being free. He had his health, a pocket full of money, and a whole gang to command. He had all of the power and perks that came along with such a position.

Sydney was a two-bit hood with no more than ten dollars in his pocket on a good day. But Dre knew his brother wouldn't let it slide. Will was teaching him about the streets, and there were such things called *principles*. Whenever principles were involved, his big brother usually felt the need to kick some ass.

"I'ma get him," Will said and was out of the car in an instant.

Dre was left with his burrito and the .45. He preferred the burrito. On the radio, Tupac had advice for brothers being pursued by their local law enforcement.

Open fire on them busta-ass bitches!

Will had to march twenty paces to catch up with Sydney. Dre watched stoically. He couldn't hear their conversation, but there were only two responses you could give when someone demanded their money.

Dre chewed his food slowly. His insides began to feel sour. Will was talking to the transient rather than hitting him. That was good. But Sydney made no attempts to reach into his pockets. He held his hands to his sides and then outstretched in a *Who me?* gesture. Sydney then pointed down the street to where his pot of gold was buried perhaps. Will's arguments grew louder. A few curse words made it back to the Cutlass. Dre turned the radio down and took a deep breath. Sydney took a right cross to the jaw and promptly crumpled, as if he'd been shot.

Dre sighed. He didn't know what to feel. On one hand, Sydney was a loser; a drug addict who did nothing but beg and steal and get high – making the community look bad. But he was still a *person.* He had relatives who loved him and was born beautiful, just like everyone else. But watching Will in action was something special. He may not have got his GED while locked up, but Will certainly got his *nigga-whoopin-degree.*

He told Dre things were primitive in the pen. With no guns, you had to get good with your fists. You had to get better than other inmates who'd been in there practicing for years. Will was now *really* good. You couldn't even see his hands move when he fought. He bobbed and weaved like a prairie dog with a hawk on its ass.

Sydney's mistake was popping back up like a Jack-in-the-box after every blow. Dre wondered why he didn't just play dead. The cocaine in his system made him either numb or dumb. With the radio down, Dre could hear them now.

"C'mon, Will, I–"

WHAP!

"I swear I'ma get it, man. I got–"

WHAP!

"Listen! *Please*, Will! I ain't lying! If you let me make it over here, I got–"

WHAP!

Sadly, Will wasn't even fighting him, not really. He had a good thirty pounds on the dopefiend and could have easily knocked him out. He toyed with him instead; hitting him with open-handed blows. Will feigned like he was going to throw a right hook and then clocked him with a left when Sydney tried to block. Will hunched his shoulders, making Sydney react for a jab, and then caught him with an uppercut to the gut.

"Where was you finna go?"

"*Nowhere, G. I swear man!*"

"You was finna score from Reggie and them?"

"*Naw, Will. No, I wasn't! I ain't even got no money!*"

"Where my money, man?"

"G, I got you. Please. I–"

WHAP!

"You said you was coming back Tuesday!"

"*I tried, Will. I came. You wasn't here, dog. I swear!*"

"Fool, you know where I be!"

WHAP!

It was broad daylight. Dre marveled at his brother's daring. At eleven in the morning, Will stood on one of the busiest corners in the city and whooped the tramp like Sydney was his child. He looked back at his Cutlass and yelled something to his little brother.

Dre pretended not to hear. Sydney took this moment of distraction to flee, but Will kicked his legs from beneath him, almost nonchalantly.

"C'mere!" he yelled again. "Hurry up, Dre. Come whoop this nigga for me!"

Dre hoped Will didn't say what he thought he heard. This would be the third fight Will tried to get him involved in since he got back from the joint. Dre kept telling him that fighting really wasn't his thing. But Will said that was akin to *homosexuality*.

"C'mere, nigga!"

Dre reluctantly got out of the car. He didn't immediately rush to the foray. He didn't have to. Will had Sydney by the collar. He dragged the tramp to the Cutlass almost effortlessly. Sydney reeled like the scarecrow from the *Wizard of Oz*. He fell, got dragged on his knees, made it to his feet, rode an imaginary bicycle, and then fell again.

"Come on, man," he begged. "*I can get it!* If you just, if you just. *Hey!* Let me go, Will. I'll pay you. *Don't do me like this.*"

When they reached his car, Will threw the dopefiend at Dre's feet.

Sydney didn't know who to plead to. From his knees, he begged both brothers for leniency.

"Just let me go around the corner. I can get it in *five minutes.* I swear. I got a dollar fifty right here. *Take it.* I can get you eight-fifty more, right around the corner. I can, I could get you ten. *Ten* more! *Fifteen* more! Just let me go, man. I don't want no more." He spoke quickly, rambling and drooling.

Sydney's eyes bugged. He looked like the LAPD had been at him. In just one minute, Will had given him nasty bruises about the eyes and mouth. Blood flowed from his nose. Dre thought Sydney might have lost a tooth, but there were a few missing already, so it was hard to tell.

"Dre, you heard me calling you. Whoop this nigga for me."

Will was breathing a little heavy. He stared at his brother with contempt but not serious anger yet.

Dre tried to back away from them. His rump encountered the Cutlass.

"Naw, man. *Please* don't hit me no more." Still on his knees, Sydney turned to Dre. His spooked eyes sought compassion. He held his hands up. His fingers trembled. "I can't get no money looking like this, man. I *steals* for a living. I can't go in no store. They call the police. *Stop, man.* Listen. I got you. Let me make it, lil homey. Don't hit me, man. *Please* don't hit me."

Will kicked him in the side, and Sydney fell flat on the pavement.

"Shut up, cuz! Say, you better hit this nigga, Dre!"

"Will, I..." Dre's heart was like a speaker box in his chest. His mouth was dry. Will saw this, and his eyebrows knotted over his nose.

"Dre. Hit this nigga."

"Don't hit me man, I–"

"Shut up, cuz! Kick him or *something*, Dre!"

"Will, I don't wanna..." Dre still had a burrito in his hand. He squeezed it so hard, the innards spilled from it.

"Don't kick me, man!"

"Shut up, I said! My little brother *is* gon' kick you. Either that, or I'ma knock yo ho ass out. Which one you want?"

"Don't kick me in the face, then. *Please.* I gotta go in stores. Get some money."

"Dre, if you don't kick this nigga *right now*, I'ma beat *yo* bitch ass. Quit acting like a goddamned *mark* all the time! You make me sick with that shit, cuz. I *swear* you make me sick!"

Dre kicked out and caught the junkie on his shoulder. It wasn't very hard, but Sydney was a good actor.

"*Oww! Man, that hurt*! He got me! See? He did it! *He got me.* Let me go, Will. I'll, I'll go get yo money–"

"Kick him again, Dre. That didn't hurt."

"It *did* hurt, G. I ain't gon' lie to you. I never lie to you. I done learnt my lesson, Will. You ain't gotta *do* me like this in front of everybody."

"Kick him again!"

Dre booted harder this time and tagged him on the same shoulder. Sydney squealed and got his whole body into the act this time. He fell to his side and grabbed the injured arm.

"*Oww*! He got me, man! He got me *good,* Will. It *hurt* too. Let me go, G. He got me."

"Kick him in the *face*, Dre."

"*No*! Not in the face, man. I gotta go in the store!"

Dre's face twisted with emotion. He felt his eyes watering, and he knew Will would hit him if he cried. Dre dropped the burrito and balled his fists. It was never going to be enough. He drew back, and when Dre kicked this time, he seriously tried to punt Sydney's head from his body.

It was a perfect shot; right on the temple. Upon impact, Dre felt like he jammed his big toe. He heard an unusual sound, somewhere between a *crack* and a *squish.*

Sydney didn't have to feign injury. His head snapped to the side, and his body followed, sending him into a roll that looked like break dancing for a second. He wobbled to his knees, rubbed his head, asked his mother for five dollars, please and then fell face forward. He looked dead, but his breath stirred the dirt around his mouth.

Dre's heart tried to squirm up his throat. Will hadn't seen anything greater since Tyson took a piece of Holyfield's ear. He laughed and pointed.

"*Hell yea, cuz*! That's what I'm talking 'bout! You shut that nigga up, Dre. Look at him, man. *He gone*. That's the first nigga you knocked out?"

Dre nodded numbly.

"Look at him, cuz! Don't that make you feel *good?* To see you can shut a nigga down like that – that don't make you feel *good*? Quit looking like that, man. You can't be looking like a ho when you fuck somebody up. You still look *soft*, like you finna cry or some shit. We gon' get that *sensitivity* up outta you, Dre. Get in, nigga."

Dre stared at the body for a moment and didn't notice his brother was ready to pull off.

"Get in, *cuz*. Somebody gon' call the law. Can't have nobody laying in the parking lot like that. People gon' think he dead."

Dre's legs were wet noodles, but he managed to get back into the car. Will exited the parking lot without speeding and turned Tupac back up. Six blocks away, Dre told him his foot hurt. Will said that was the dumbest shit he could have divulged. Of all the emotions running through his mind, Dre picked the *sissiest* one to articulate.

Will said the toe comment cost him any respect the knockout may have garnished. Dre would have to knock out somebody else to get that respect back.

CHAPTER TWO
COLLEGE BOY

Chris crossed the main lawn of Texas Lutheran with deliberate swagger. He wanted to look menacing and confident. He had no friends at the university. A detailed search was not needed to conclude that he was one of very few black faces on campus that day. It was summer time, though. Chris figured there would be more students of color come fall, but he doubted their population would reach more than ten percent. By the time he made it to the administration building, he caught himself subconsciously playing *Count the Black People*. His high number was two.

The July afternoon was hot but not unseasonably so. The heat index would rise to 110 degrees later in the month, and August was like a fart from hell, so the 96 degrees today was actually nice. The students Chris came across wore shorts and sandals. Only a few carried books. Most of them lived on campus with little care about anything going on past the school's perimeter.

Chris wore a royal blue tee shirt that hung down to his thighs. His khaki Dickeys were starched stiff. His Chuck Taylors were blue. The shoe strings were blue as well. Chris' skin was dark with a hint of red, like rosewood. He wore a neat crew cut with no beard or moustache.

Despite the clean shave, he knew that his overall appearance conjured the word *THUG*. That was fine with him. Chris didn't know that the security guards at Texas Lutheran had been chasing *thugs* from their campus for years. But if he had known, that wouldn't have been a deterrent. Chris liked the fact that he was the only person at the school who dressed that way.

≈ ≈ ≈ ≈ ≈ ≈ ≈

Texas Lutheran University was an oddity of sorts. Founded in 1923 as a women's college, the campus was once nestled in the heart of a thriving neighborhood. The area had a good mix of blacks, whites and a few Hispanics. The black and Hispanic kids were bussed to segregated schools in those days, but the community got along fine. It was a working class neighborhood. People greeted each other with a friendly *How do you do?* And they always kept their yards neat.

The neighborhood was nick-named *Poly* because of the only high school in the area; Polytechnic High. Actually, this school was the source of the area's decline. In 1971 integration came to Overbrook Meadows, and all of the residents could finally send their kids to the closest school.

Coincidentally, at this time most of the white parents decided they would rather their children went to private schools, or at least schools in *whiter* neighborhoods. As the white families moved out and the property values went down, more blacks and Hispanics eagerly filled up the vacancies. But even without the Caucasian residents, it was still a superior neighborhood.

Poly remained a nice place for another fifteen years. It was crack that changed things. A lot of minority neighborhoods in America went downhill in the 80's, so no one complained much. There are now parts of Poly that look like Beirut and sound like Bagdad after dark.

The one thing the whites couldn't take with them when they fled was their prized university. So Texas Lutheran, still in pristine condition, is nestled in the heart of what is sometimes described as *madness* by local reporters – and rightfully so.

Chris grew up in Poly, so when he stepped onto the private property of the university, it was a totally different world. White people with nice cars, professors with briefcases, and sheltered kids named Shellie and Chad were literally blocks away from dope houses where twelve year old soldiers toted .380 automatics and sold crack by the ounce.

The security guards at Texas Lutheran might believe Chris was defiling their elite property with his *ghettoness*, but Chris felt like he was bringing Texas Lutheran a more realistic portrayal of its community. Even better, he deserved to be there.

Looking at him, you would never guess Chris was an exceptional student who could count the C's he made on his high school report cards on one hand. You wouldn't believe his scholarship was *not* athletic, and you certainly wouldn't think he was a pre-med major, but that's what was printed on the registration card he handed to the portly woman in the administration office.

Chris thought she would comment on his choice of majors, maybe try to redirect him to an easier field of study. But the clerk was professional.

"Looks like your financial aid packet is complete," she told him, handing his card back with a smile. "See you in the fall."

And that was it. Chris was officially a college student. He left the building with his spirits high. He still wanted to look thuggish, but couldn't stop smiling as he skipped down the steps and returned to his car.

≈ ≈ ≈ ≈ ≈ ≈ ≈

Chris exited the parking lot and headed south on Lutheran Road. He went two blocks and made a right on Rosedale. Like the whole Poly area, Rosedale had once been a great roadway. Now there was more graffiti than entrepreneurs on the decaying strip and more potholes than promise.

After a five minute drive, Chris entered the Evergreen Terrace Apartments on the south side of town. The complex was a sprawling 90 unit catastrophe enclosed by a length of fence that was ten-feet-tall and topped with razor wires. The razor wire was stretched, compromised, and completely removed in several sections, and the natives cut a number of holes in the chain link fence at strategic locations. These holes were so regularly traversed, there were trails leading to and from them.

Chris often wondered if the idea of the fence was to keep the residents safe or to keep the city safe from the residents, because anyone breaking into Evergreen Terrace had better pack a lunch, an Uzi, and a platoon if possible.

The fence was hideous, but it was just the beginning of the apartment's disrepair. The lawn surrounding the buildings stood high enough to conceal a legion of basketballs. Abandoned units were either left open or broken into, usually by prostitutes and their Johns or dopefiends looking for a quick scavenge.

Apartment management at the Evergreen was nonexistent. Technically, the residents had been between managers for two months now. There were no maintenance people to call for leaky faucets or regurgitating toilets. When the last manager abandoned the venture, most of the residents who were seriously concerned about their safety left shortly afterwards. There were only a few residents there who still dropped their rent off in the night box. Everyone else had been living rent free, taking advantage of the situation until someone came to shut the place down.

In the meantime, Evergreen Terrace was run by a set of Crips. The gang had basically renovated the place to better suit their needs. Any knucklehead bold enough to roll past the front gates was guaranteed to get exactly what he was looking for, whether that was a beat down, a good high, or a good fuck. The AGG Land Crips had two leaders; both were ruthless and organized and a clear hindrance to Overbrook Meadows' Gang Unit. OG Will was dark and menacing. OG Kody was well-schooled, but he was just as frightening.

No pre-med student or any college student would find comfort within the confines of the Evergreen, but Chris was an exception to many rules. The parking lot there had potholes as bad as Rosedale, so his Plymouth Reliant crept slowly at a driveby pace. Chris pulled up to building F and parked next to a Fleetwood with shiny, twenty-inch rims.

From his car, he saw a crowd hanging out on the breezeway upstairs. There was always a lot of activity in or around apartment 4F. This wasn't necessarily the place to go for guns, drugs or stolen goods, but all of those things were filtered through this unit.

The whole complex was home turf for the AGG Land Crips. Apartment 4F was their central control room. The leaders met here to discuss the gang's moves. Large amounts of cocaine, marijuana, and heroin were brought here, broken down, and distributed to the many runners. This is also where members of the gang hung out and got high and bonded with the people they loved more than their own family. Chris didn't know what to expect in apartment 4F on any given day.

There were four people on the breezeway. Chris only recognized one of them. Dante was Kody's right hand man. He was overweight at 240 pounds, but it didn't look so bad because he wore most of the bulk in his chest and arms. Dante was known for his one-punch-knock-out abilities. Chris had the pleasure of seeing him in action a few times.

Chris had known Dante for years, but he still got greeted with, "What you doing here, nigga?"

"Nothing."

"Ain't nobody in there but Greg," Dante said, announcing more to his comrades than to Chris that it was alright for this guy to go in.

Like most gangs, the AGG Lands Crips used a specific handshake as a greeting. Chris passed the four gangsters on the breezeway without giving them the handshake because, despite his attire, he was not a member of the gang.

They continued their conversation as he passed.

"So this ho ass nigga gots *two* straps, but I ain't scared of that bitch. I tells him..."

≈ ≈ ≈ ≈ ≈ ≈ ≈

Dante's depiction of the visitors inside the apartment was inaccurate. At first count, there were at least *eight* people in the living room and kitchen area. Chris suspected several more might be lurking in the bed or bathrooms. Three of the occupants were women. They appeared to be either sleepy or drunk or high off unknown toxins. Dante most likely mentioned only Greg, because he and Chris had become really close lately.

Deuce, the youngest member of the gang at 13, was wowing the crowd with his ability to slaughter militants on his Xbox. Deuce had a huge afro that was admired by all. Anyone could grow hair, but his mother was Hispanic, and he had that coveted *good* hair. There was only one television in the living room. Chris was surprised that the grown men and women relinquished it to a video game. But they were enthralled, as if it was a movie.

Two rough-looking men sat at the dining table. They were cutting a flat slab of dope into chocolate chip-size morsels that

175

would go for ten dollars a pop. A couple of the females watched them with clear interest.

Greg sat on the apartment's only loveseat with a baking sheet covered with marijuana on his lap. He was in the midst of his trademark activity, which was something Chris rarely saw him go more than a few hours without doing. Five fresh blunts were already assembled. He looked up at Chris with a delightful twinkle in his eyes.

Greg was tall and thin. He skin was fair, his hair long. He could've passed for Hispanic, but his mother was actually Caucasian. Greg had a large, slightly pointed nose that made his long face look even skinnier. Overall, most people thought he resembled a rodent. The struggling whiskers under his nose furthered this illusion.

"What up, my nigga? Say! Come here, boy!" Greg waved Chris over. One of Greg's bunny-rabbit teeth was slightly askew. He looked like a young child sitting there; his thin legs meeting at the knees to support the pan.

Chris found a metal folding chair behind the sofa. He set it up next to his friend. Chris was grinning broadly himself. Greg was somewhat of a psychopath, but Chris liked him a lot. Greg was the comedian of the crew. He wasn't a good fighter, but he could have a roomful of people rolling with just his expressions. Chris used to wonder if that was the only reason they kept him around.

"What's up Greg," Chris said as he studied the herbs. "I see you still at it."

"*At it?* What, *this*?" Greg held up a blunt and stroked it under his nose like an expensive cigar. "Nigga, this shit ain't no hobby. This my motherfuckin *life*! I thought you was starting school. Didn't you say you was going today?"

The girl sitting closest to them was eavesdropping. She grinned at Chris. He returned the smile, but he wasn't interested in her at all. Most of the women who frequented that apartment were *boppers.* These were women who liked to get high and preferred to go out with drug dealers because they had a steady supply of cocaine and heroin, also known as *girl* and *boy.*

"I only had to register for classes today," Chris explained. "School doesn't start 'til August."

"Say," Greg said, "you my motherfucker!" He was in a festive mood. "Hey!" he yelled to the crowd gathered around the television. "Say, y'all, this mothefucker going to *college*! This nigga finna be somebody! Ain't you, Chris?"

Chris' smile faltered as the thugs turned to give him a once over. He had too much melanin to blush, but his face flushed with heat.

The girl he smiled at said, "For real?" and a few others told him that was, "Tight." But for the most part they didn't give a damn about his aspirations. If Greg announced Chris had just robbed a convenience store, he would have garnished more praise.

"Say, Chris, watch me put this rocket launcher on these ho ass niggas!" Deuce yelled over his shoulder. The crowd erupted in cheers as a projectile flew from his character's weapon into a swarm of digital enemies on the other side of the screen. Video games were getting too realistic. The explosion was followed by plenty of carnage. Glad the attention was off of him, Chris looked back to Greg.

"So, what you gon' major in?" Greg asked.

"I told you I was pre-med, nigga. You didn't believe me?"

"I thought you was bullshitting, cuz." Greg traced the length of a sixth blunt with his tongue. "So you really gon' be a doctor? Nigga, you that smart? You know them Chinese motherfuckers got that shit sewed up."

Chris didn't correct his friend about how it was actually the Vietnamese and Korean students who were excelling in American schools. He downplayed his status: "Man, I'm smart enough."

Finished for now, Greg placed the last blunt on the baking sheet and leaned back in his seat. He presented the blunts to Chris.

"Get one, nigga. I *know* you gon' get high today." Greg's smile was almost maniacal.

Chris had made it all the way through high school without touching the wacky tobacky. But two weeks ago, after much prodding from the likes of Greg, he took a few puffs from his first illicit drug. Much to Chris' disappointment and Greg's bewilderment, he didn't get high at all. A few days later he tried again with the same results. Greg said a lot of people didn't get high off weed until their third or fourth experience. At the time,

Chris wondered why anyone would try a third or fourth time if it didn't work the first two.

Getting high was something Chris made a rational decision to do, and it was pretty much going to happen. It had nothing to do with peer pressure. His brother kept him out of gangs, and his mother made sure he took all of the accelerated classes at school. Outside of his electives, Chris hadn't been in a classroom with *regular*, neighborhood kids since the fourth grade.

Now that he was going to college, Chris felt like he was being pushed further and further away from what it meant to be young and black in America. He wouldn't recognize the ignorance of this thinking for years to come. In the meantime, he wanted to get high, like everyone else.

"Say, nigga, you through?" a cocoa-colored hood called G-Roc wanted to know. G-Roc was one of the roughest members of the set. He was a great fighter and a ruthless adversary for his foes, but he was not well respected in the clique.

G-Roc was the only member of the gang who had to be reprimanded for wearing dirty Dickeys and scuffed sneakers too often. And he was gaining a reputation for being untrustworthy because he often came up short with his drug pedaling. This was most likely related to his increasingly destructive *boy* habit. But snorting heroin was casual for a lot of members of the gang, so no one called him on it... yet.

"Hell naw, cuz," Greg told G-Roc. He was still smiling. *Always* smiling. "The first one's going to *college boy*! This nigga finna be a *doctor*! Get you one of these, Chris." Greg's eyes were warm and nurturing. He could have been Grandma offering a fresh batch of peanut butter cookies.

"Hell yeah," someone said.

"Celebrate that shit, nigga!" another shouted.

"Chris finna get *blowed*!"

The room erupted in adulation for the corruption of the one pure homeboy they had left.

G-Roc sneered and said, "Man, fuck that ni–" He caught himself before anyone heard him. If any member of the set disrespected Chris in that manner, the consequences wouldn't be nice. They didn't have to like him, but they would tolerate and respect him. G-Roc knew it. Everyone knew it.

With all eyes on him, Chris selected one of the skimpier blunts from the baking sheet. Greg caught the move and wasn't having it.

"Hell naw, *nigga*. Get that *fat* one!" Greg motioned with his nose, which was looking more and more rat-like.

Chris replaced the skinny and took the fatty. He held it uncomfortably and looked around. Everyone watched him with amusement, except for G-Roc. G-Roc looked like he wanted the fatty.

Embarrassed, Chris said "I don't have a..."

"Here you go." One of the boppers produced a blue King lighter.

Chris accepted the lighter and looked to his mentor. Greg licked his lips. Chris lit the tip of the blunt and sucked slightly until an ember manifested. The cigar was grape-flavored. A racket of coughs erupted from his lungs as his body rejected the foul air. With tears in his eyes, he looked around and saw that everyone was pleased with him.

With the formalities over, the gang rushed forward to snatch up the remaining cigars. Chris bobbed and weaved to avoid the arms reaching around his head. Greg was the only one who sat motionless.

"Yo, hit that shit again," Greg urged. "You finna get high for real! This popcorn weed!"

Chris inhaled again, slower this time, and he managed to hold most of it in. A little smoke got in his eyes. He winced at it, wondering what the hell *popcorn weed* was.

CHAPTER THREE
HIGH LIFE

The third time proved indeed to be the charm.

With the blunts gone, the atmosphere in apartment 4F shifted from energetic to the nonchalant boredom that sapped the drive to do anything creative or productive.

Deuce traded exploits on faraway battlefields for a far more comfortable fetal position on the floor. He snored softly and looked younger than his thirteen years. Three people lounged on the sofa, and Chris noticed it was a really nice couch, considering the environment. Expensive, black, and leather, it could go for $2,500 brand new. But a particularly desperate dopefiend sold it for four dime rocks one rainy night.

G-Roc left the apartment an hour ago in search of a sneaky Mexican gentleman who supposedly owed him money over a series of fixed dog fights.

"Nigga, you ain't finna get shit off them eses," one of his comrades warned him on the way out. But G-Roc lurched on with haggard determination.

Greg lounged on the loveseat. He sank so deeply into the cushions, he appeared to be in danger of breaking his neck. He used the cap of a discarded ink pen to excavate some of his ear wax. He looked down his nose and studied each clump he retrieved. Chris couldn't help but chuckle at him.

Greg eyed him lazily. "Man, your eyes red than a motherfucker."

Chris squinted at Greg, as if seeing him for the first time. "Nigga, you look like a rat," he said.

Greg grinned. "Aw, fuck you nigga. You *high*, cuz. I told you that shit was some–"

"Naw, naw. I'm for real," Chris went on. "You got, like, these beady eyes. And your nose–"

"Chris–"

"Your nose, it's like–"

"Chris–"

"It's like – what man?"

"Nigga, you *high*!" Greg insisted. "You high as hell, cuz."

"I'm not." Chris took a few moments to assess his faculties. "Well, I'm..." Slurred speech, eyes wanting to close though not really sleepy. "I guess I..." Looking around, the room swam in a slow-motion fashion that was not indicative of sobriety. "Yeah, I might be..."

"Fuck that might be shit. Chris. Listen: You high."

"Yeah. I'm high," Chris conceded and laughed.

"Shit's funny, ain't it?"

"Man, I don't know. It just seem like..." He chuckled.

"You got the giggles and shit."

"Yeah. Everything's just so, *funny*."

"Yeah. That's how it be when you first start smoking." Greg was an expert on the subject. "You be like, thinking everything funny and shit. Then sometimes you be getting paranoid; thinking everybody trying to fuck with you. But then, after you been smoking that shit for so long, you just be like, *cool*. Stuff still be funny, but not like it was when you first started."

"I guess, 'cause right now you really do look like a rat."

"Fool, that's that weed talking. I don't look like no damned rat."

Chris shook his head. "Uh uhn. I remember, even before I smoked that blunt, you already looked like a rat, a little bit. But now everything's like, you know, *magnified*. I can see it better now..."

"Say, fool..." Greg's smile faltered.

"Damn, Greg, you *do* look like a rat."

Chris didn't know the girl was still there until she spoke. Her eyes were low and red. She wore a pair of tight Capri's with brown sandals. Chris hadn't noticed before, but the ass and thighs stuffed in those pants were thick and enticing.

"Ho, I don't look like no motherfucking rat." Greg's smile was completely gone now. A homey clowning you was one thing, but he'd be damned if he'd take it from some hoochie.

"But you got those little whiskers," she said, pleased that she'd gotten a rise out of him.

Chris cracked up.

Greg looked back at him with a flicker of resentment, and then his high-yellow features softened and morphed back into his characteristic grin. He winked at Chris and then spat fire at the girl.

"Fuck you, bitch! You look like a damned *drive through*. You know how many niggas done ran up in this bitch, Chris? You have to count them on all your fingers and all your toes – and that's just the ones she fucked this week! She don't even know they real names. *Boon. C-Loc. Tay. Mack.* What's Mack's real name, bitch?"

She twisted her lips into a sneer but didn't respond.

"It's *Daryl*, ho! *Daryl Jeffries*. We gon' start calling your ass *Stop N Go*."

Chris laughed.

"Fuck you," the girl said, but her ego was wounded. She piped down.

"Say, Chris, you hungry? Let's go get something to eat."

Greg sat up and stretched. "Let's get some hot wings or something."

Chris rolled his eyes dreamily. "Man, I ain't going nowhere. I'm not hungry."

"Yeah you is, cuz. Get up, old lazy ass nigga." Greg stood and ruffled Chris' hair as he passed.

"I ain't trivin – I mean, I ain't *driving*," Chris said.

"Fool, you can't even *talk* right. I sure as hell ain't finna let you drive me nowhere. Get up, cuz!"

Getting up proved to be easier said than done.

"You want something, Stop N Go?" Greg asked on the way out.

"Fuck you," the girl replied.

≈≈≈≈≈≈≈

Outside, the blistering sun felt good for the first few seconds as it warmed their bodies. But by the time they made it around the side of the building, Chris felt beads of sweat on his forehead. Greg marched ahead of him. He ducked under one of the holes in the fence and waited for Chris to catch up.

"Man, what's wrong with you?"

"I don't know. It's hot out here. Why you want to go now?" Chris stumbled over a protruding root and nearly fell.

"What, cuz?"

"I told you, I'm... Say... Greg?" Chris ducked through the hole and shook his head. "How I'm supposed to enjoy this, if I'm trekking all over the city?"

"What, cuz?"

"I said, how you niggas be getting high and going all over the country and shit?"

"Chris..." Greg put a hand on his shoulder and looked into his eyes. "You know you sound retarded right now, don't you?"

"I'm just saying," Chris pondered. "If y'all be getting high all the time, why you wanna be going all across the country, if you already got you an established high spot?"

Greg laughed. "Cuz, I have to ask you to think about what you saying before it get out your mouth."

"I told you I was messed up."

Greg continued to laugh at him. "I know, Chris. But you done took it to another level. What the hell you talking about *Star Trek* for? You done got on some *science fiction* shit!"

"I didn't say nothing about *Star Trek*."

"You did, cuz. You said we was *Star Trekkin*."

"No I didn't," Chris explained. "I said we were *trekking* to this dumbed, I mean damned store."

"What the fuck is *trekking*? That still sounds like some *Star Trek* shit to me. That's the only time I done heard that word."

"To '*trek*' means to travel, Greg." Chris tried to moisten his lips, but there was no saliva available. He didn't remember trading his salivary glands for cotton balls, but apparently that was the case.

"When you be taking hikes through the woods..." Chris went on. "I'm just saying, we giving, I mean, we going a long way to this damned store. I don't understand how y'all be getting high and then go on hikes and stuff. That doesn't make sense to me.

The air conditioner in the apartment was blowing real nice..." He wiped his brow.

"The store is right there, Chris." Greg pointed at a building no more than fifty paces ahead of them. "You high for real, cuz. Try to cool that shit out before we get in there."

How does one cool out a high? Chris considered this but didn't come up with a solution before they made it to the building. His inebriation was immediately evident when he tried to enter through the OUT door. He shoved it more than once, wondering why it wouldn't open.

That's odd. Greg just walked in ahead of him through the same door. Wait, no he didn't. Greg went in through the door on the right. Chris smiled at his mistake. He entered through the correct door and stood bewildered. Now Greg was nowhere in sight.

Sam, the proprietor of the establishment, eyed the lanky youngster with amusement. "Greg, this nigga's *fucked up*. What you do to him?"

Sam was of Middle Eastern decent. He grew up in the States and fully absorbed the Ebonics of his community. The first time he met him, Chris thought Sam took his familiarity a little too far. But he learned to accept Sam for what he was. The store owner was in his early twenties. He talked black, dressed black and liked a big, round booty as much as anyone else Chris knew.

"He on that corn," Greg called over his shoulder.

Chris stood on his toes to look over the aisles. He saw that Greg was patronizing *Sam's Grill.* On the south side, a lot of the corner stores were capitalizing on the Negro's love for fried foods, and their willingness to acquire these rations from the most convenient source.

Only in the hood can you get gas for your car, malt liquor, jewelry, games for your Xbox, Robitussin, diapers, antifreeze *and* a pork chop sandwich all in the same place. At Sam's you could also get Salisbury steaks, sausage on a stick, collard greens and pig's feet. There was no end to the non-black hands eager to help black people part with their money.

"You been smoking popcorn?" Sam asked.

Chris looked over at him and shrugged.

Sam wore a striped Polo shirt with baggy jeans. His sterling silver necklace caught a few eyes, but not as much as his

Movado. Sam's bling might have made him a target in this neighborhood, but his demeanor and reputation warranted respect. He was a good friend to have. He paid lowlifes to clean up around the store, and occasionally he let the dope boys duck inside if the police were on to them.

"You know, I just got out of jail two days ago," Sam hollered at Greg.

Greg ambled over to the counter and leaned on it with both elbows. "Yeah, I heard you shot somebody, Sam. What you do that for?"

"You remember that motherfucker I told you was stealing 40s?"

"Yeah."

"This motherfucker keeps coming in here. I see him. I'm watching him. *Every day* he keeps coming in here and don't buy shit." Sam looked from Chris to Greg.

"So the other day I'm *waiting* on this motherfucker. He comes in here and does the same shit. I'm busy with customers, so I don't watch him the whole time. But when he gets ready to leave, he don't buy shit.

"I'm pissed off 'cause I missed him, but later that same night he comes in again. This time, I watch him go to the beer. I open the register and start counting money, like I don't see him. But out of the corner of my eye, I'm watching his ass the whole time. He take out a forty, look around, and then put that shit in his coat; under his arm." Sam looked from Greg to Chris again.

"A forty, you know, ain't shit. Just a dollar-fifty, right? But I don't really make shit in this motherfucker. I buy that forty from the vendor for a dollar and get fifty cents profit. That's it. He steal one, that's a dollar-fifty gone, so I don't get no profit off the next three I sell. I got bills man. My electric bill last month was twenty-three hundred dollars."

"Damn!" Greg said. "Just from the lights?"

"Well, I got all the signs and shit. Plus I leave the lights on overnight. Then I got that kitchen, but that ain't the real problem. The problem is this motherfucker stealing from me *every day*. Two, three, four times a day. So, I'm watching this asshole."

Chris sighed. He wanted Sam to stop looking at him.

"I wait for him to come to the counter, and then he walks up. I give him a chance to pull that shit out and pay for it, but he don't. He keeps walking. So when he gets to the door, I pulls out my shit. You know I keep this motherfucker right under the counter." Sam produced a hand-cannon.

"Shit!" Greg shrieked and backed away from the counter.

"I don't even say shit to him, just **BAM!**" Sam pointed the piece as if shooting. This totally unnerved Chris, who was standing close to the imaginary line of fire. He ducked, drawing a chuckle from the store keep. Sam put the gun away.

"I ain't gon' shoot you, motherfucker. Anyways, the first bullet went in the wall over there by the door. I shot again and hit him in the shoulder. He fell into the door and pushed it open. I ran around the counter and caught up with him in the parking lot, and then I beat the hell out of him!"

"You whooped him?" Greg asked, his eyes wide. He loved violent stories.

"Hell yeah!" Sam's eyes were wide and frenzied, too. "Then I looked up and saw this other fool in the car waiting on this idiot. So I'm thinking, *You been driving this motherfucker to my store to steal? And you drinking my beer, too?* So I got off the one I shot and ran over to the other one. I reached his car and tried to drag that motherfucker out, but he holding on to the wheel too hard. So I just start beating his ass, too."

Chris shook his head. This was impossible to believe.

"Man, I fucked up my knuckles in that nigga's mouth!"

Sam held up his fist and showed off the wounds. "By then, the first motherfucker done managed to get in the passenger side, so the driver starts backing up with me still hanging in his car. I said, *Fuck it*, and let them go. They take off down the road. You wanna know the *fucked up* part about it?" Sam asked Chris directly.

Chris shrugged, and Greg said, "What?"

"Them niggas get to the hospital and call the police on *me*! They wanna press charges on *me*! Can you believe that shit?"

It made perfect sense to Chris, but he didn't say so.

"The police came over here and arrested me. I had to close the store and everything. They was talking about charging me with attempted murder. You know the only thing that saved me?"

Chris had no idea.

"You paid 'em off?" Greg was dead serious.

"The one I shot was still *inside* the store. If he was outside, I'd be fucked. Ain't that some bullshit?" Sam was genuinely annoyed that he couldn't defend his fifty cents profit with deadly force. "In my old country, you steal from somebody, they chop off your hand. You rape somebody, they cut your dick off. They don't play that shit where I come from."

Chris smiled. Sam's accent only came out when discussing his roots.

"They still charged me with assault on the guy outside. But my lawyer say I can get probation for that. Ain't that fucked up?"

Chris didn't know what to think. He was really uncomfortable, though. Greg's laughter was maniacal.

"Anyway, what y'all getting?" Sam asked.

The hell up out of here, Chris thought.

Greg paid for 24 spicy hot wings.

≈ ≈ ≈ ≈ ≈ ≈

Back at the apartment, Chris didn't think he had much of an appetite. He was wrong about that. Greg told him he had the munchies. Chris knew what the munchies were. He didn't think that was it, but damn if those weren't the best hot wings ever. He ate twelve of them and then lounged on the couch and laughed his ass off at one of Greg's tales from the hood. Chris knew a good deal of Greg's anecdotes were totally fabricated, but that was okay. With an attentive audience, Greg spun one hell of a yarn.

They talked for a couple of hours. Sometime towards the end, Greg stopped in mid-sentence to confront Chris.

"You sleep, nigga?"

Chris mumbled that he wasn't and politely succumbed to slumber.

CHAPTER FOUR
KODY

Chris awoke to the clamoring of thugs who usually achieved their greatest level of degradation after nightfall. Other than Greg, there were only two people in the apartment when Chris fell asleep. Disoriented, he squinted as he looked around the living room. The loveseat Greg sat in was now occupied by the thick girl in Capri's. *Stop N Go*, Chris thought, and smiled. Deuce was at the dining table bagging up more marijuana than Chris had ever seen. He scooped fistfuls from a garbage bag that was almost half full.

There were new arrivals, too. Spooko, wheelchair bound from a baseball bat to the spine, was there, and so was Moon. Moon was over forty; an old man compared to everyone else. He was finally back on the streets after a routine traffic stop went terribly wrong 25 years ago. When the dust settled, a deputy required facial reconstruction surgery. Moon got shot four times during the incident, but he lived to tell the story.

There were plenty of lively characters there, but only one person garnished the attention of the *whole* posse. People levitated to this guy. They surrounded him and exchanged greetings. They exchanged money with him and sought his approval. He pounded fists with them.

The man wore black and blue. His hair was recently braided into seven tight corn rolls. They hung down past his hairline like snakes. He wore a neatly-trimmed goatee. The white of his eyes had a permanent shade of pink. And though (or possibly because) his skin was darker than any of the Amistad crew, the neighborhood hoochies couldn't get their panties off quickly enough when he looked their way. OG Kody was the well-respected and equally despised co-founder of the AGG Land Crips.

Kody scanned the room purposefully. His expression was nonchalant at first. But when his gaze fell upon Chris, his eyes darkened. It was a quick look that no one else noticed.

Kody wore a blue tee shirt with black Dickey pants. His blue Chuck Taylor's had thick, black shoe strings. Chris loved to watch him interact with people. Kody's exploits made him an icon, yet there he was. Tupac in the flesh.

There were places in the city where voicing your allegiance to OG Kody would garnish immediate respect. There were also places where voicing that allegiance would guarantee you an ass-whooping, or worse. Chris knew Kody better than anyone in the room, but he still found himself caught up in the grandeur.

Kody finally broke away from his homies. He gave Chris another hard glare and yelled, "C'mere, nigga." He turned and walked out of the apartment without looking back, because, when you're OG Kody, you know people are going to do what you say.

Chris got up and yawned. He stretched slowly, trying to give the impression that if he was leaving, it was because he wanted to do so. A couple of thugs were grinning at him, shaking their heads.

Outside, darkness had come. Time-activated bulbs glowed and hummed throughout the apartment complex. Moths and mayflies bounced off the dingy lamp covers. From the breezeway, Chris looked down on Riverside Dr. and he thought he could see for miles. It was like their ghetto version of the Las Vegas Strip.

The breezeway was deserted except for Kody. He stared at Chris for a few moments before pouncing.

"Cuz, what you doing over here?"

"I came to see you." Chris looked away coyly and couldn't stop a smile from curling his lips.

"You didn't come to see me. You would've left when you seen my car wasn't here. You came to see *Greg*, nigga."

"I didn't even know Greg was up there until I got here." That was the truth, so Chris was able to maintain eye contact.

"Whatever. You knew *somebody* was gon' be here to get you high."

Chris' jaw dropped. Kody was like one of those nosey, helicopter parents. He liked catching his little brother off guard.

"Oh, you didn't think I knew you been smoking? What's wrong with you, Chris? Why you wanna fuck with that shit?"

"I was just—"

"Just what? Man, that ain't even *you*, cuz. You a *nerd*, Chris. You go all the way through high school without messing with drugs, making straight A's and shit. And now you wanna experiment?"

"Weed ain't a real drug," Chris replied. "Everybody smokes weed." That slipped out without much forethought, and he regretted it immediately.

"It's niggas in there snorting raw and boy too, cuz. You wanna put something up your nose next? Plus, I keep telling you, *'This ain't no motherfucking hangout!'*" Kody was serious now; stern eyes with his lips curled. "It's all kinds of stuff in there. It's *crack*, Chris. *Guns.* Everybody in there taking penitentiary chances, and they know it. What makes you think this is some place to hang out?"

"I wanted to see you," Chris said, and there was truth in that.

Kody softened a bit. "Yeah, but what if the laws run up in there while you sleep on the couch? What you gon' do then? You ain't going to college if this motherfucker gets busted and you up in there *chilling*. You know that, don't you?"

"I don't have no drugs on me."

"When they ran up in that house on Jessamine, they found two ounces of crack," Kody informed. "It wasn't in nobody's pocket, so everybody chilling in there caught a case."

A breeze rustled the leaves of a nearby tree, and the dry branches clicked together. They sounded like old bones. The scent of something dead drifted up from the fence line.

"I hardly ever get to see you," Chris said. He was glad they were alone, because comments like that could set you up for a season of ridicule, even if you were talking to your brother. "You never come by the house. Those people be around you all the time. You even spend the night over here." Chris lowered his eyes for effect. It almost worked, but Kody followed his gaze.

"What the fuck you doing with that shit in your shoes?"

"They just shoe strings."

Kody was flabbergasted. "Chris, what the hell is wrong with you? You wanna get shot? You can be—" He paused and then snarled. "You better take them shoe strings off. Soon as you get home, boy. Don't never wear them shoe strings again. You a *school-boy*, Chris. You won't even know what to do when some niggas roll up and ask what set you claiming. We got enemies, cuz. Niggas wanna kill us. I don't know what part of that you don't understand, or what you think is cool about it, but you..." Kody shook his head. "Say, go home, Chris. Just, *go home.*"

Chris conceded. Kody was right, as usual. He never missed an opportunity to push Chris away from his criminal lifestyle. Chris knew that his brother was trying to help, but he would never stop wanting to be around him. It hurt him to see that Kody loved the people in apartment 4F as much as he loved his real family. Chris turned and headed downstairs to where he left his Plymouth.

"Say," Kody called after him.

Chris glared over his shoulder.

"You need to chill with that weed, for real."

"It's just weed," Chris said without stopping.

"Alright then. On the way out, ask one of those crack heads what drug he started off on. For real."

≈ ≈ ≈ ≈ ≈ ≈ ≈

Chris didn't see any crackheads on the way out. But he did pass OG Will as he exited the complex. Will drove a black Cutlass with dark windows and shiny, black rims. Most debates about who was the tougher leader of the AGG Land Crips ended undecided. But Chris always gave the edge to Will. Both leaders were dangerous, resilient, and pretty damned ruthless. But Kody had a heart, and it was common knowledge that Will did not.

Through the window tint, Chris could barely make out the occupants of the Cutlass, but he thought he saw Dre's afro bobbing in the passenger seat. Chris didn't know of a case where an apple fell so far away from the tree than with OG Will and his brother Andre. Will stood 6'2, while Dre mustered a mere 5'7. Will was fresh out of the penitentiary and cut up like Holyfield in his prime. Dre was chubby with plump cheeks, wide hips and a round belly.

Their personalities were also flagrantly different. A few months ago, without the help of any psychology handbooks, Will decided he could fix the problem. He enrolled his little brother in street school. The only course available was called, *Get That Bitch up Out Ya*. OG Will was the teacher. For their lessons, Will took Dre with him everywhere he went.

Dre didn't like apartment 4F, but he had to go multiple times each day. And Dre didn't like drivebys, but Will made him ride shotgun, literally. Any deviations from Will's idea of *macho* resulted in discipline.

Will tongue-lashed his brother publicly for low-level infractions. His scathing rebukes were so ugly, Chris would've taken a swing at him. But Dre merely lowered his head and reflected on his inadequacies. Will slapped the back of Dre's head more times than Chris could remember. Chris once saw Will attack his brother, delivering hard blows to the arms and chest rather than the head. Chris was also there when Will pushed Dre down the second half of a stairway.

Anyone paying attention knew Will was getting nowhere. But no one intervened. Two months into the experiment, Dre was still timid. Some would argue even more so. Yet Will pressed on with dogged determination. At this point, everyone was waiting for something to snap. Greg joked that Dre might one day use one of Will's guns against him, like in the movie *Full Metal Jacket*.

Chris made a left on Riverside and headed home.

TO BE CONTINUED...

ABOUT THE AUTHORS

Keith Thomas Walker, known as the Master of Romantic Suspense and Urban Fiction, is the author of a dozen novels, including *Fixin' Tyrone*, *Dripping Chocolate* and *The Realest Ever*. Keith enjoys reading, poetry and music of all genres. Originally from Fort Worth, Keith is a graduate of Texas Wesleyan University. Visit him at www.keithwalkerbooks.com.

Phyllis Wonjou Allen, a fourth generation Texan, is deeply rooted in the story-tellin' tradition of her Hood County family. Her mother, Ella Allen, encouraged her to create a rich fantasy life of characters and playmates in her head. It has only been in the last few years that those characters have moved from the playground inside her onto the pages of published works. Phyllis has published quite a few stories, including *The Red Swing*, *Piano Lessons*, *Mama Minnie*, *Shopping Trip*, *Blood on the Moon*, *The Unintended Consequences of Our Brothers* and *The Crown*. Phyllis has won the Kente Cloth Short Fiction Award, the University of Mary Hardin Baylor's Best Short Fiction Award and a Katie Award from the Press Club of Dallas.